STORIES
of the
CONFEDERATE
SOUTH

STORIES

of the

CONFEDERATE SOUTH

Rickey E. Pittman

PELICAN PUBLISHING COMPANY
GRETNA 2007

First printing, 2006
First Pelican printing, 2007

ISBN-13: 978-1-58980-518-7

The characters and events in this book are fictitious. Any similarity to real persons, living or dead, is coincidental and not intended by the author.

"Lily" was first published in *Ceili,* March/April 2005,
Deo Vindici in the *Confederate Veteran,* Vol. 62. Sept./Oct. 2004.

Printed in the United States of America

Published by Pelican Publishing Company, Inc.
1000 Burmaster Street, Gretna, Louisiana 70053

"The real war will never get in the books."

—Walt Whitman

Table of Contents

STORIES
of the
CONFEDERATE
SOUTH

Deo Vindici

I am a Southerner…
I won't apologize
I won't be reconstructed.
I will not surrender
My identity, my heritage.
I believe in the Constitution,
In States' Rights,
That the government should be the
Servant, not the Master of the people.
I believe in the right to bear arms,
The right to be left alone.

I am a Southerner…
The spirit of my Confederate ancestor
Boils in my blood.
He fought
Not for what he thought was right,
But for what was right.
Not for slavery,
But to resist tyranny, Machiavellian laws,
Oppressive taxation, invasion of his land,
For the right to be left alone.

I am a Southerner
A rebel,
Seldom politically correct,
At times belligerent.
I don't like Lincoln, Grant, Sherman,
Or modern neocon politicians like them.

I like hunting and fishing, Leonard Skynnard,
The Bonny Blue and "Dixie."
I still believe in chivalry and civility.

I am a face in the Southern collage of
Gentlemen and scholars, belles and writers,
Soldiers and sharecroppers, Cajuns and Creoles,
Tejanos and *Isleños*, Celts and Germans,
Gullah and Geechi, freedmen and slaves.
We are *all* the South.

The South…My home, my beautiful home,
My culture, my destiny, my heart.
I am a Southerner.
Deo Vindici.

Just Another Confederate Prisoner

The vilest deeds like poison weeds
Bloom well in prison-air:
It is only what is good in Man
That wastes and withers there:
Pale Anguish keeps the heavy gate,
And the Warder is Despair.

—Oscar Wilde

When my father died in Afghanistan, I think my mother lost her mind. Most nights, she'd get crazy drunk at the Backdoor Lounge, and even though she got two DUI's, she didn't let up. The drinking gave her a mean side, too. One night just after last call, a man called her a drunken whore, so she sliced him a couple of times with a straight razor. It's hard to imagine one's own mother, her eyes glazed and hard, standing over a whimpering, bleeding man like she was a Southern belle avatar of blood.

One night she brought a man home. He spent that night, and the next, then the next thing I know, he's moved in with us. I know my mama's entitled to have a life, and it's not her fault that my Daddy's Army Reserve unit was attacked, but I still didn't cotton to the man being around. I don't think my daddy would have liked him either.

The next morning, I fixed myself some grits and sat down at the table, leafing through that month's *Civil War Times* magazine. He stumbled into the kitchen.

"Coffee's made. Help yourself," I said.

His eyes were bloodshot, and he stunk like stale beer. "What on earth are you eating?" he said.

"Grits. Want some?"

"Hell, no. I can't believe some of the things you Southerners eat?"

Oh, great, I thought. *Mama's taken up with a durn Yankee.*

"Yeah, we're Southerners. Where are you from?"

"Iowa. You heard of it?"

I stood and stacked my dishes in the sink. "Yeah, that was one of those Yankee states that wouldn't let any black folk live there during the Civil War. I guess its citizens weren't fightin' to free the slaves."

After he left for work, Mother joined me in the kitchen. She was in a tear, scrambling around, fighting her way into her work clothes. I poured her a cup of coffee and set it on the counter. I asked her, "When is this new boyfriend of yours going away?"

"Jim's not leaving. We've decided to live together."

"You're kidding me. Daddy hasn't been buried two months and you want to shack up with this freeloader?"

"Don't you get pissy with me, Joseph. You make our relationship sound trashy."

"I don't have to make it sound trashy—it is trashy and you know it is."

"Well, he's not going to leave. We could move into his apartment, but our house is bigger. We've even talked about getting married."

I looked at her ring finger—saw a white strip of skin where my daddy's wedding band had been. I wondered where she had put it and when she stopped wearing it. "I think you've lost your mind. Must be in some kind of midlife crisis."

"Well, if you don't like that information, you'll like this news even less—we're moving next month."

"Where to?"

"Davenport, Iowa."

"I don't want to go. I want to finish school here."

"You're only sixteen, so you *will* go. The West Monroe Rebels will do fine without you. When you're seventeen, I'll sign for you to get out on your own and you can do what you want. What do they call that? Oh, yeah, I'll *emancipate* you. Now, get your butt out the door and get to school without getting another tardy."

My daddy and I were members of the Sons of Confederate Veterans. That night, I attended our January camp meeting, and before the meeting sat down with our camp commander, Mr. Porter.

"Y'all have been real supportive since Daddy got killed in Afghanistan, and I want you to know I really appreciate it, but I got some more bad news. Mama says we're moving next month to some end-of-the-world place called Davenport, Iowa. So I guess this will be my last meeting till I can find my way back down here."

"Joseph, I hate to hear that," the commander said. "But I guess it's the Lord's will. Why are you moving? Did State Farm transfer your mother?"

"Naw. She's got this Yankee boyfriend now. It looks like they're going to get married and he's put it in her head how much better her life will be up there. He's got a high-dollar job with some construction company. He talked her into asking State Farm for a transfer. She got it fairly easy, so I reckon it's a place with lots of jobs or it's a place that no one else wants to go to. I don't know what I'll do up there."

"Well, for one thing, you can see Rock Island, the prisoner of war camp. Remember me talking about it a few meetings ago? It's on an island in the Mississippi, right between Davenport, Iowa and Illinois. Go see it as soon as you can, while it's winter. That way you can see what our boys went through there. Take some pictures and send them me. I'll put you in touch with a SCV group that does a lot of volunteer work for the Rock Island Park. You can attend their meetings. You'll probably help the cause more there then you will here. Who has your mama taken up with?'

"Someone named Jim Lane."

Mr. Porter shook his head. "That's ironic. A Yankee general from Kansas had the same name. His men were the Red Legs that ravaged Missouri."

"I guess his ghost has come to Louisiana. I don't like this man. My daddy would have never made me move to a Yankee state. Think you can keep me on the roster? I'll be back in a year most likely. Maybe I can talk Mama into letting me come down to march in the Mardi-Gras parade."

"You'll stay on our roster. You stay in touch too. As soon as you get me your new address, I'll send you our newsletter. And if you ever just need to talk, you know you've got friends here, so call me any time. We Southerners have to stick together, don't we? I know moving away doesn't feel right, but you still have to do the right thing and go with your mama. *Deo Vindici.*"

After the meeting, the camp took me to the Cheniere Shack restaurant, bought me a farewell supper, and gave me a battle flag. One by one, the men stood and told stories about my father, how he was a true Confederate, and talked about how proud I should be for being his son.

I was.

*   *   *

Davenport, Iowa was as bad as I feared. School was worse. The first day of school, the principal called me into his office.

"I wanted to welcome you to our school, Joseph."

"Thank you, sir."

"Sir. Now I haven't heard that word from a student in quite a while."

"You ought to move to Louisiana. You'd be sirred all day long."

"Joseph, I've been looking at your file. You have excellent grades, but I need to ask you about something. In the student parking lot, there's Toyota pickup with Louisiana plates and a Confederate flag hanging in the back window. I assume the truck is yours?"

"Yes, sir, it is. Why?"

"Well, I'm going to ask you to not display the Confederate flag in your truck on school property. You'll also need to scrape off your Confederate bumper stickers."

"Why?'

He looked down, shook his head and smiled. "You're a bright boy. In this enlightened age, do I really have to explain?"

"If you want me to take them off my truck you do."

He blew an exasperated sigh.

Oh, boy, I thought. *He's gone from condescending to pissed.*

"We can't allow any racist symbols to be displayed on school property." He glanced at my T-shirt with a battle flag on front. "Or on clothing either."

If he could have read the words to "I'm a good ole Rebel" on the back of the shirt, I figured he'd really have a conniption. "That rule doesn't make sense to me. If people interpret the Battle Flag as a symbol of racism, they need a history lesson. Do I look like I'm a racist?"

"I'm not saying you're a racist. It's just—we can't and won't allow such symbols. Since you're a new student, I'll cut you some slack today, but after today, I don't want to see any more Confederate symbols on your clothing or your vehicle."

"Well, I guess I'll have to follow your dress code, but I'm not going to change the way my truck looks. I suppose I can walk or take a bus to your school."

"This is your school, too, Joseph."

"No, sir, it's not. I didn't want to move here. In Louisiana, our school mascot was Johnny Reb, a rebel soldier. I was always proud of that."

"Well, I'd suggest you adjust to the way things are here. Iowa is not Louisiana. You can go back to class now."

I stood. "No, sir, it's not Louisiana for sure." I left, less than excited about Davenport Central High School whose sports teams were once called "The Moon Men" and then "The Imps."

When I left school, I parked my truck in front of our house. Jim Lane was sitting on the porch, and a forest of beer bottles bristled on the end table next to him. He rose when I stepped out of my truck and wobbled toward me.

He looked at me with his bloodshot eyes and shouted, "What's wrong with you?"

"Sir?" I said. "I don't think nothin's wrong with me, but you sound as drunk as old Abe Lincoln again."

"Your principal called. He told me all about the conference today in his office. He said you were belligerent. I told him I was not surprised, but I'd straighten you out and take care of the situation." He stood, opened a pocketknife and walked to the back of my truck. Bending down, he scraped off the Confederate bumper stickers.

I watched the little symbols of my ancestors peel off and drop to the ground. The wind tumbled and skidded the Bonny Blue and the SCV logo fragments down the street.

"You ain't got a right to do that," I said.

"Right? Listen, you little shit, I've got the right to do whatever I want. This truck's in your mother's name, not yours.

And she'll go along with whatever I want. Unlike you, she's grateful for what I've done."

"You got the power, but you ain't got the right. You know, once you start drinking, you get a real mean streak."

"Shut up, you stupid cracker. I'm tired of hearing you talk about all that Confederate crap. Get that flag out of your back window. I'm tired of seeing it. I'll not have anyone see it and think I approve of it. It's embarrassing. I wouldn't be caught dead in a vehicle with anything Confederate on it."

"That's good, because I sure wouldn't want anyone thinking you were a Confederate like my daddy was."

I saw his fingers knot up in a fist. "You'd better quit running that mouth of yours so much." He grinned in the way that drunken people do. "I'm your daddy now."

I knew I was getting close to a deadline, so I turned without a word and walked inside. My mother was ironing, but her face was red and streaked with tears, and I saw a bruise on her arm the size of a Yankee's hand.

"What's wrong, Mama?" I asked.

"I'm alright."

"No, you're not. Is he beating up on you?"

She looked at her arm. "No. It was an accident."

"Yeah, sure. I guess you heard your boyfriend carrying on about my truck. I don't know how much of him I'm going to be able to take."

"Jim means well, Joseph." She set down the iron and wiped her nose with her shirttail. "Please, try not to anger him."

"The durn fool stays mad, Mama. Christ, I feel like I'm being attacked by some anti-Confederate Gestapo."

"You better get your flag out of your truck before he does. He can get ornery when he's drinking."

"Alright, but only to make things easier on you. As a matter of principle, I oppose the idea. I'll hang it in my bedroom in the morning."

I went to my room and completed my homework, then sewed some C.S. brass buttons on my Carhartt coat, wondering if anyone would notice, but I wouldn't have been surprised to learn that the Davenport School District had some button law, like some towns did during Reconstruction. I fell asleep reading a biography of Jefferson Davis. I found my flag the next morning on the living room floor—cut up in eleven pieces.

* * *

That Friday night, I called the local SCV camp commander. His name was William Cain.

"I was expecting you to call. John Porter's already called and told me about you. I'll do my best to keep you from getting too homesick. Louisiana's loss is our gain. You want to take a little outing tomorrow? I thought I'd take you to Rock Island. It will be cold, so dress warm. It will be an experience that you'll never forget."

He was right.

The next day, he picked me up and we drove to the island prison and I filled him in on my circumstances.

Rock Island is located in the Mississippi River, directly between Rock Island/Moline, Illinois and Davenport, Iowa. From the Moline Bridge on the Iowa side, I could see the river circling the island like a giant moat.

It was the first prisoner of war camp for Confederates I had ever visited, an ugly part of the War Between the States that I'd never really thought about. We walked through the museum, studying the pictures and artifacts, and talking. I saw a fiddle that a Florida soldier named Purdee had made, and a dove that another prisoner had carved from a mussel shell. Then we moved outside and strolled through the grounds. William rehearsed the prison's history, and pointed out the locations of the original stockade and other buildings. We stopped in front of one of the barracks.

"There were eighty-four of these 100 x 20-foot board barracks. Each barrack housed 120 men. The men slept in triple-deck bunks. The barracks weren't much bigger than some mobile homes in Louisiana. My ancestor was in barrack no. 36.

"Twelve thousand of our boys were confined on these twelve acres," he told me. "It was so easy to die here. Disease, cold, and hunger, they all took its toll on our men. The South lost about 2,000 good men here. And think about it—this rotten place was the last place on earth many of them saw. They never said goodbye to their families—they never even heard if they had won or lost the war.

"Most of them had never been in a place so cold. It gets down to thirty below zero some days. They never had enough blankets, and they slept two or more to a bunk. Smallpox spread through the camp for a while. A doctor here, a good man by the name of Clark, tried to build a hospital, but the Commissary-General of Prisons, Colonel W. Hoffman, considered a special hospital for prisoners to be an extravagance and put a stop to it."

"How did they survive?"

"Same way you will. Gritted their teeth, thanked the good Lord for every day they survived, ate what was set before them, which wasn't much and what they did get often wasn't fit to eat."

"The Yankees had plenty of food. Why wouldn't they feed them?"

"Andersonville. In response to reports of conditions there, the Federal government cut the rations of all secessionist prisoners. Some Christian women in these parts were horrified at the plight of the prisoners, and brought food and clothing, even though the military officials ridiculed and insulted them for doing so. Soon, by government order, even that charity was stopped. A Tennessee boy, Charles Wright, said that the order came from the Commissary General of Prisoners in Washington, dated August 10th, 1864. It practically cut the prisoners off from the outside world and all hope of assistance. There were to be no more food from friends, no more flour from the sutler, no more clothing, no prospect of prisoner exchange, no hope of early release, and no more visitors. Some soldiers wanted out of Rock Island so badly they took an oath of loyalty to the Union and were sent out West to fight Indians."

"What would you have done?" I asked. "Would you have taken the oath?"

"I think I would have tried to hold on and make it out alive. But I know I'm not as tough as our boys were, so I really don't know what I would have done. Cold and hunger can hurt a man bad, not just physically, but on the inside too."

After we entered the Confederate cemetery, he led me to a particular grave.

"Here's what I really wanted to show you. This was my ancestor on my mother's side of the family."

I read the markings on the pointed gravestone, no. 599.

YOUNG, JOHN   PVT   E   28 ALA   2/24/64

"He was shot by a guard for trying to use the sink at night. I've thought about moving his body away from here, back home to Alabama. But I don't know. Maybe it's best his body stays here. Where's your ancestor buried?"

"In Louisiana somewhere. He died at Port Hudson." I looked at the neat rows of crosses, and I knew that a big hunk of the Confederacy's heart was buried here. "I like this place, but I hate everything else up here."

"How old are you, Joseph?" William asked.

"Sixteen. And when I'm seventeen, I'm lighting out back to Louisiana."

"Some of the boys here were close to your age. A number of them died here. Many were here for nearly two years. You've got a hard row to hoe, Joseph, but they had it worse. If they could make it through this hell-hole, you can make it too."

We ambled through the cemetery and William told me story after story about the men buried here, stories that angered me, and stories that broke my heart. He pointed out the graves of two men thought to be Confederate ancestors of President Clinton and Vice President Al Gore. I couldn't help but think that if those politicians had bragged about their Confederate ancestors they would have acquired more votes from the South than they did.

That night, I refused supper and went to bed hungry. And I didn't eat the next day neither. One night, the temperature reached thirty below, and I closed the heat vents, opened my bedroom window, and shivered through the night under one single blanket. I know it wasn't the same thing our Southern boys went through in those winters of 1863-64, but it made me feel something I hadn't felt before, and caused me to understand some things about the war and myself I had never really thought about.

I made it through that cold night all right, and I made it through the next year of school. Next week, I'll be seventeen, and I'll be given the parole that will cut me loose from my own Rock Island prison sentence. I hate leaving my mother behind in this God-forsaken place, but I know she's a prisoner too. She never should have surrendered to that Yankee invader of our family. She'll have to find her own way home, and when she gets fed up with his crazy rules, when her heart gets tired of the emotional cold and hunger, I know she will. She'll realize what she is to Mr. Jim Levin—just another Confederate prisoner.

Jasmine

These should be hours for necessities,
Not for delights; times to repair our nature
— King Henry VIII

F rederick O'Connor woke to the touch of a woman's hand. Delicate fingers lightly stroked his hair and rubbed the nape of his neck. The rain fell in a steady patter, thumping the window of the *Chartres Street* crib.

"You best wake up, soldier boy," the woman's voice said. "It's nearly noon. I done let you sleep here in my bed as long as I can. I got to get me some sleep. You can come back tonight and see me if you want."

Frederick lay on his stomach, his face buried in the lumpy feather pillow. He rolled over and through bloodshot, burning eyes looked at the woman.

The woman sat on a slat chair next to the bed. Her mussed, blonde hair was pinned to the top of her head. Her blue eyes were sparkling and mischievous, her cotton nightgown faded and worn. Her legs were crossed, and when she lifted the gown's edge to scratch her porcelain-white thigh, Frederick's heart raced. *She favors Erin,* he thought. *That's why I keep coming to this woman.*

"You were a wildcat last night, soldier boy," she said. "Spending those greenbacks on me in the saloon like you was a wealthy planter. I never seen a man so drunk before! And talk, Lord, you rattled on all night about that prisoner of war camp you was in. You was too drunk to walk after I brought you here, and I just didn't have the heart to throw you out on the street like most would have done. Some women would have emptied your pockets and some might have done worse than that, you being a Yankee and all, but don't you worry none. You still got

14

all your money other than that you gave me. You best be grateful that I felt some goodness left in you. I bet you got yourself a mean hangover."

"What did you say your name was?" Frederick reached for his trousers that were hanging on the bedpost. He dug into the pockets and touched the roll of bills, just to make sure it hadn't been pinched, though he couldn't remember how much money he had started the night with. Nor could he recall how much he had spent on this woman.

"You *are* a curious one," the woman said. "You been with me here all night, and still don't know my name. It's Jasmine."

"Jasmine?"

"Jasmine. It's not my real name, but that's what my Seamus called me. He always said I was his pretty little yellow flower. You can call me Jasmine if you want."

"Who called you Jasmine?"

"Seamus, my husband. At least he was my husband till he joined the 6th Louisiana Regiment and got himself killed at Gettysburg. Now I ain't got no one to look after me but myself. But, pshaw, I told you all this last night. Don't you remember?"

"I been here all night?" he asked.

"Mostly," she said. "After we left the saloon, we came here and you drank a jar of tafia and passed out. You still want me to cut your hair? You said so last night. I can cut a man's hair so it looks nice and proper. Only cost you another dollar for me to do it. Ain't no trouble at all."

Frederick felt the bile of last night's liquor curdle in his mouth. A dense fog swirled his thoughts into an incoherent mush, and sharp throbbing jabs of pain clawed at his brain. "No, don't bother. I'll find a barber."

"Most barbers here in New Orleans would as soon cut a Yankee's throat as cut his hair," she said. "Southerners have long memories. Best let me cut it, darling."

"No, I said." Frederick rose to his feet in the room's twilight and studied his wobbly legs, still withered and spindly from dysentery, the months of poor food at Camp Ford, and the long marches to Shreveport and back to Tyler and then back to Shreveport as a prisoner of the Confederates.

"I hope you ain't leavin' New Orleans no time soon," Jasmine said. "You should stay for the festival. Ain't but a week away. I bet you ain't never seen nothin' like our Mardi Gras."

"I got to be on my way. I've got a wife and a ranch in Texas I have to get back to."

"That's a pity. I'd like to see you again. Since your General Butler and his Yankees invaded New Orleans, it ain't been easy for secessionist widows like myself. My sister is worse off than me though."

Frederick scanned the room. Besides the bed and the slat chair the woman sat in, the only other piece of furniture was a bureau. On its top sat a wooden lantern, its candle now a shapeless wax nub. "How could your sister possibly be worse off?"

"Polly's husband joined the 6th Louisiana the same day Seamus did. I know my Seamus got hisself killed, but her man was captured and sent to some place called Elmyra. He came down sick and died. She wrote to find out about his grave, but couldn't make sense of what the commander said in his letter. The Yankee letter said his body was taken off by some doctor to a medical school. That didn't make no sense to me neither.

"Well, after she got that news, she and her eight children were on St. Charles Street watching a Yankee funeral cortege passing by their home. Everybody was real solemn and then she started laughing and carrying on saying she was glad the Yankee was dead, and how she wished all Yankees in New Orleans would end up the same way. Then she and her children started singing "The Bonny Blue Flag." A Federal officer in the procession got real irritated and ordered her to be arrested. Said she had violated General Order 28. They took her outside the city and confined her to an old trapper's shack, and won't let nobody visit her.

"Lord, I don't know what will become of her children. They're in an orphanage now. I'm trying to save up enough money to get a bigger place so I can get them out of there. I've got nearly three hundred dollars set aside. Ever time I look at a Yankee, I think of my poor sister, living out in that ramshackle shack in that mosquito bog."

"She shouldn't have laughed and spoken ill of the dead. A man's death ain't nothin' to laugh about."

"I guess it ain't." Jasmine walked over to the bureau, picked up a brush and stroked her hair. "You're from Texas? Why did you join up with the Federals? Are you an abolitionist?"

"No, I ain't an abolitionist, and I never really cared for any I met. I joined the Army to save the Union."

"Most Yankees I talk to say they joined up to save the Union, but I can't really get none of them to explain in detail what 'saving the Union' means. Seems a lot like a man beating his wife to keep her married to him."

"It doesn't matter now what it means. I just made a decision to fight with the North, and that's all there is to it. A good number of Jack County boys joined up with me. And we saved the Union, by god!"

"You may have saved the Union, but you ruined us—probably ruined the Texas town you're wantin' to get back to. I can't rightly think that the war saved anything in the South. Most of us here lost something, some everything. And this Union you fought to save, well, my guess is folks in the future will regret you saving it. Where did you say you were going?"

"Jack County, Texas. It's west, about as far as you can go without living in Indian country."

"A Yankee Texan. Don't rightly know what to think about that. I knew you didn't sound like those other Yankees swarming New Orleans. They sure talk in a funny way, some of them. Course, I'll take a secessionist boy over a Yankee any time. They're more polite than any Yankee I been with, and they don't steal nothin' from us. Only thing is Confederate boys ain't got no money—and a lot of them are missing arms or legs to boot. I know what I am, but a Secessionist still treats me like a lady. Yankees, they all treat me like I was…"

"A whore?" Frederick said.

"Like I said. They're more polite. Now, why don't you get dressed and get your Yankee ass out of my room. I'll be glad when the whole lot of you is gone from New Orleans."

"I've been discharged from the Army. I'm going back to Texas."

"I don't care. Go on back to Texas. Go on back to your wife you been mumbling about in your sleep."

Frederick stood and shuffled over to the chamber pot in the corner. A picture of General Butler had been pasted to the pot's bottom. The stream of his water descended upon the general's balding head.

"You gonna pay me now?" the woman asked. All the sweetness and pretense had left the woman's voice.

"You said I paid you last night," Frederick replied. He picked up his trousers and shirt from the floor, shook them out, and dressed.

"You been here all night and half the day, drinking my liquor and taking up space. This place ain't no army barracks, so your stay here ain't going to be for free."

"I'll be on my way then." Frederick threw a dollar on the bed and opened the crib's mildewed rickety door. He contemplated the ankle deep water gurgling down the brick-paved street. The rain and grayness had depressed him since he first arrived in

New Orleans. Outside, a few drunken soldiers aimlessly tramped about in their wet, muddy, blue greatcoats and gum blanket ponchos. He watched the dirty blue spots weave their way in and out of saloons deeper into the *Vieux Carre*. "Damn, it rains here nearly as much as it don't rain in Texas."

The woman picked up the greenback with one hand and stuffed it into the bureau drawer. At the door, she stood on her toes so she could place her chin on Frederick's shoulder and she looked at the street with him.

"Ah, honey, this rain ain't nothin'."

Frederick watched the rain pellets strike the pavement and ricochet. A Federal soldier exited one saloon and splashed and sloshed his way across the street and entered another.

"Sometimes, it will rain hard for days," Jasmine said. "I seen the ground get so soft that coffins will pop out of the ground and float down the streets."

The force of the rain blurred the outline of the buildings just twenty feet from where he was standing. Frederick hesitated, stepped forward into the downpour, and then retreated back inside.

The woman raised up on her tiptoes again and kissed him on the cheek. "Honey, don't go out in this bad weather. I don't care that you was with the Yankees. Stay one more night with me."

Frederick realized that there was really no reason to hurry away. His steamer didn't leave for Houston until tomorrow, and if he left here, he would probably end up in another saloon, and leave with another woman like he had with this one.

"This ain't fit weather for you to be traipsing about," Jasmine said. "Texas ain't goin' nowhere. Come on back in, and I'll pour us another drink. Then I'll treat you to something really special. When the rain lets up, I'll go to the market and get us something to eat."

19

Frederick took a step back, his hand still on the doorknob, indecision pinching his face. Jasmine slipped her arm around his waist and pulled him toward her.

"That's it, doll. Stay and talk with me. It's been a long spell since a nice man talked to me, and I'm hungry for decent conversation. A woman's got a need to be talked to. And you know I'm worth every cent you spend on me."

Frederick closed the door, crossed the room and sat back down on the bed, using the wall as a backrest.

"I like you, Frederick. You just sit down here awhile, least till all this rain lets up, and I'll pour us another drink."

Jasmine uncorked another jug of tafia. She filled two tin cups and handed one to Frederick, then sat down on the bed next to him.

"Now, honey, tell me all about yourself."

Frederick felt her fingers entwine his own, felt the fingers of her other hand stroking his, pausing over each scar and callous.

"It must have been hard to have been a prisoner of war in your own state," Jasmine said.

"There's easier things to live through, I guess."

"You're lucky you got out in one piece. How did you end up here? Why didn't you just mosey on back to your home in Texas? How did you get captured?"

"If you'd quit rattling, I'd tell you." Frederick drained the tafia and held the cup out for the woman to refill.

"I was Texas Cavalry, and we and some Kansas boys were assigned to guard a wagon train in Arkansas. Must have been 400 wagons. This was in April of '64. At first I wondered why the Army would make us guard empty wagons, but as we passed the secessionists' houses on the Camden road, I understood what the wagons were for. We durn near robbed every house and farm we passed! You should have seen what we took from those arrogant secessionists—silver, quilts, jars of honey, beds, horses, jewelry—just about anything we took a cotton to.

"Well, a regiment of Rebel cavalry came on us unexpectedly. We formed a battle line to try to protect the wagon train, but they surrounded us. They took our horses and marched us to Tyler. They had a stockade there they called Camp Ford. The Western boys inside were alright, but there was also a lot of trash there from up North. Didn't care much for them. I had been to Tyler as a boy, and remembered it as a real nice place generally, but a year in that stockade sure took the joy out of any good memories."

Frederick rose to his feet and paced back and forth as he talked. "We had food and water at least, and there wasn't a shortage of company. If my ciphering is right, after the 2,000 prisoners from Mansfield came, there were nearly 5,000 of us in that stockade. Weren't many Texans like myself inside, but there were a few. "When the war ended, the Rebs didn't let us go like we expected. They marched us to Shreveport. We'd walk all day, then sleep at night in cornfields. We looked like a bunch of ragged scarecrows. Must have been a sight.

"At Shreveport the secessionists turned us over to Federal officers. Well, our own army didn't let us go neither. They said we had to go New Orleans to get discharged. So, they herded us onto a leaky steamboat they had captured on the Red River and hauled us to New Orleans.

"Once we reached New Orleans, an officer slapped me on the back and said, 'Soldier, you should be happy you got out of that hellhole prison camp. Don't you have anything to say?'

"Do you know what I told him? I said, 'What the hell am I doing in Louisiana? And how soon can I get out of this damn idiot army?' "

Frederick laughed, turned and looked at the woman. She had fallen asleep and was snoring, gentle as a mewing kitten. Her hand still loosely clasped her empty tin cup.

He snickered. "Most folks work sitting up and sleep on their backs."

Frederick walked to the woman's bureau. He reached into the drawer and took the bundle of bills inside, folded them and stuffed them into his pocket. At the door, he turned and whispered, "Yep, Jasmine, you were worth every cent I spent on you."

The Taking of Jim Limber

My fault is past. But, O, what form of prayer
Can serve my turn? 'Forgive me my foul
murder'?

—Hamlet

I t's near dawn. I stare at my letter until the words swirl on the page. Setting my pen on my desk, I close my eyes and bury my face in my hands, listening to the rain pound the windowpanes like an idiot beating a drum. The laudanum's euphoria has faded, and once again peaceful sleep has eluded me. Jim Limber's ghost claws at the ragged nerves of my conscience, surfacing in the dark river of thoughts that drift without mooring and swirl in the undertow of the night's silence.

I whisper, "I was a soldier, Jim Limber. A soldier follows orders. I did what I was told. I did what they wanted. Leave me be...Leave me be."

But I know he won't.

I crumple the letter I've written, walk to the fireplace, and toss it into the flames. The wad of rag parchment opens as if the fire wishes to read and absorb my confession, and its crackling tongues hungrily consume ink and paper, truth and history.

My eyes drift to a faded newspaper clipping on my desk, a letter of Jefferson Davis pleading for information of Jim Limber's welfare. My thoughts are dragged like a prisoner of war back to Savannah.

We had deposited Jefferson Davis in Fort Monroe, and returned by steamer to Savannah where we placed his wife Varina and the Davis children under house arrest. I had been assigned sentry duty. Throughout the day, secessionists with sad

23

and angry eyes strolled by the shrine, hoping for a glimpse of the Davis family.

The unforgiving Georgia rain lingered as relentlessly as rebel opposition had in Virginia. I slung my tampion-plugged Springfield over my shoulder with the barrel pointed to the ground and bowed my head. The water streamed from the brim of my black slouch hat like a flooding creek, and in spite of the oilcloth poncho, my uniform was drenched, and it clung cold and heavy upon my shivering skin. The weather and the curfew finally drove the Savannah pilgrims to their homes, and I was left alone in the humid Savannah night.

Turning my head, I gazed into the open window behind me and studied the Davis family, strangely moved by this tableau of a traitor's family. I heard Mrs. Davis and the children talking.

"Do you think the Yankees will come back in our house tonight, Mama?" Maggie asked.

"If they do, it cannot be helped," Mrs. Davis replied.

One of the Davis boys said, "Mother, you don't think that Yankee captain meant what he said about taking Jim from us, do you? Are they going to execute us? What's going to happen to father? They don't really have him in chains, do they?"

"Hush, Jeff. Don't talk about such things. We must place our faith in God."

"Mama, would you read to us?" Maggie asked. "I think it would make us feel better."

"Yes, certainly. Bring me my Bible, Maggie."

I edged closer to the window.

Mrs. Davis opened the Bible and read, "But the wicked are like the troubled sea, when it cannot rest, whose waters cast up mire and dirt. There is no peace, said my God, to the wicked…"

The rain intensified and muted her voice, and the thick drops pounded the wooden shingles of the house like a drummer thumping the devil's tattoo. Down the street, boots carelessly splashed through puddles, the traveler's horseshoe taps scraping and slipping on the brick-paved street.

I raised my eyes and studied the shadow-man staggering and weaving toward me. Steadying himself on a hitching rail in front of the house, he lifted a candle lantern, which cast a yellow nimbus above his head. The mustached phantasm growled, "Private!"

It was Captain Hudson. I wiped the water from my eyes with my hand, and in the light of the lantern observed that he had shed his uniform and donned a suit he had taken from the Davis' Negro yesterday. "Sir!" I shifted my rifle to shoulder arms and snapped to attention.

"As you were, soldier."

"Aye, sir." I slung the rifle back onto my shoulder. As the captain peered into the Davis window, the sour smell of corn mash wafted through the thick air. I knew our captain was fond of spirits, and I also knew that liquor fed his meanness. Yesterday, Captain Hudson came to the Davis' quarters drunk, and he had rifled through Mrs. Davis' few remaining clothes. His sodden eyes had gazed so longingly at the various women's garments he pulled from the trunk, I was suspicious that he might want to wear them.

"The prisoners are shecure, private?" Captain Hudson said.

I resisted the urge to snicker at his slurred speech. "Yes, sir."

"Why are you standin' in the rain?"

"It's my post, sir."

"Your post, yes. Well, your discipline is commendable." He put his hand on my shoulder. "Son, I'm relocating your post to inside this fine Southern house. Follow me."

Captain Hudson entered the Davis home without knocking, and I followed him inside. Mrs. Davis, in a chair close to the fireplace, had set her open Bible aside and was mending a shirt. The Davis boys were sprawled on the floor playing with a few clay marbles, a wooden top, and a whirli-jig, while the girls sat on the floor near their mother's chair with their dolls.

I thought about my brothers who had fought with the Confederacy in Kentucky. It had been two years since I last heard from them. I wondered if they had made it home safely, wondered if Federal troops entered their homes in this same intrusive manner.

Mrs. Davis set the shirt in her lap and looked at us. "A gentleman would have requested entry into my home before barging in. What do you want this time? You've already taken everything of any value."

One of the Davis boys said, "Maybe he wants another dress."

"Jeff, you hush that," Mrs. Davis said. "How can we help you, Captain?"

The captain walked to the fireplace. His boots were thick with mud, and he left a dirty trail on the hardwood floor. He picked up a daguerreotype on the mantle, studying the image of the house's former occupants. "For tonight, the sentry's post has been moved from outside to inside." He slipped the silver picture frame into his trouser pocket.

"We have so little room and privacy as it is," Mrs. Davis said. "We're not going to attempt an escape. Surely it is not necessary to have him inside our living quarters."

"Even so, he will move inside." Captain Hudson glanced over at the Davis children. He fixed his dark eyes on the little black boy playing with the Davis children.

"Every time I come here, I see that darkie playing with these white children," Captain Hudson said. He looked at me. "What do you think of that, private?"

Being from Kentucky, I had seen black and white children play together many times, but the tone of his question caused me to reply cautiously. "I don't rightly know, Captain." I had hoped his *schadenfreude* would be dormant tonight, but I could tell from his eyes that the meanness had already set in.

Captain Hudson stepped over and twirled a finger in the boy's long curly hair. "Are you one of the Davis slaves, boy?"

The boy had just spun a top. His eyes followed the spinning cedar cone until it wobbled and finally toppled over. He pushed the Captain's hand away from his head. "No, sir. I've already told you once before. This is my family."

"His name is Jim Limber," Varina Davis said. "So please address him in a civilized manner. He's part of our household, and no concern of yours, sir. We are his legal guardians."

"You sure talk uppity for a prisoner."

"*Tempora mutantur et nos mutamur in illis,*" Varina said.

Jeff gathered the boys' scattered marbles together for another game. "That Yankee doesn't know any Latin, Mama," he said. "I can tell by the blank look on his face."

Jim Limber laughed with the other children. "I know what it means." He stood and struck a pose as if he were on stage. "Times are changing, and we change with them." He bowed several times as the Davis children applauded.

The captain's face flushed. "Come here, boy." He motioned to Jim Limber with his hand. "I said come here, boy."

Jim stood and cautiously approached him.

"You're a bastard slave child of Jefferson Davis, aren't you?"

"Must you be so crude?" Varina said. "My children are present, in case you haven't noticed."

Captain Hudson pulled at Jim's shirt. "Mighty fine clothes for a field hand to wear. He's contraband. I think I'll take him from you. Maybe I'll give him to someone who will teach him to hate you and the South." He sat in an armchair, popped a Lucifer with his thumb and lit a thin cigar. A plume of smoke twisted its way across the room, then spiraled toward the high ceiling. He said to Jim, "Take off your jacket and shirt. I want to see what they've done to you."

"Even a villain like yourself would not resort to such barbaric behavior," Varina said. "Why can't you just leave us alone?"

Jim Limber cast Varina Davis a puzzled look.

The captain sat in a chair. "I said, take off your shirt and jacket or my guard will do it for you."

The boy complied.

Captain Hudson twisted Jim Limber around and examined him, poking each scar on Jim's back. "Jeff Davis did this to you, didn't he, boy!"

"No, sir. Mister Davis never hurt me."

"I don't believe you."

The captain rose and dragged Jim across the floor. The little boy resisted, kicking and flailing his arms at the captain. His screams mingled with the cries of the Davis family.

"What are you going to do with our little Jim?" Varina asked. "Please, let him go." Her children scrambled over and clung to her.

"You will never see this darkie again, lady," the captain replied. He roughly pushed Jim toward me. "Take him outside, Private."

My hand latched onto the boy's bare shoulder, and I yanked him toward the door.

Jim Limber struggled to free himself from my iron hand. He began to cry and kicked me in the shin. "Mama! Mama!"

I winced from the kick, and then savagely boxed the boy's ear. "Be still, damn you!"

Mrs. Davis strode toward me. "You're not taking my little Jim."

I heard Captain Hudson draw and cock his pistol.

"Don't try something foolish," he said. "Not a word more, madam, or more of your family will go with him. And I'd just as soon shoot you as look at you."

He closed the door behind us as we left. The heavy oak door only slightly muted the weeping of the Davis family. "I'll take the boy now," he said.

In spite of the captain's orders, I felt awkward returning inside, so I resumed my earlier post in the rain. I watched Captain Hudson drag the struggling Jim Limber into the darkness.

The door opened and the oldest Davis boy shouted, "The Yankees have taken Jim Limber! Jim! Jim! Our father will find you, Jim!" His cry echoed through the empty Savannah streets.

Mrs. Davis appeared at the door. Her lips were tightly drawn together and her eyes bored into mine like a pair of one-penny nails. She rested her hand on Jeff's shoulder and gently pulled him inside. The rain resumed and intensified its attack, peppering me like rebel canister.

* * *

My captain, after he sent telegrams to several politicians he knew, was commissioned to journey to several cities and to exhibit the boy as one of Jeff Davis' slaves. I was appointed to accompany him. Our first stop was a small theatre in Washington. The auditorium was filled to capacity with Washington socialites and politicians delirious from war fever and the North's victory.

Captain Hudson strode to the podium and cleared his throat. "As you know, Jefferson Davis is safely imprisoned, in chains and under constant guard. When he was captured, we noticed this young black slave in his household. Upon inspection, we found upon his body visible signs of abuse. Private, bring the boy forth so the audience can see for themselves."

I led Jim Limber by the hand to the center of the stage. "Take off your jacket and slowly turn around."

Jim's eyes were lifeless now, the vacant eyes of a captive whose mind is numbed by his circumstances and who has surrendered to his fate. He slipped off his jacket and slid his suspenders down his shirtless shoulders. When he turned, the crowd gasped as the scars on his bare back glowed beneath the quicklime white beam of the followspot.

"Ladies and gentlemen," Captain Hudson said, "on this boy's back you can see the evil fruits of slavery. What kind of monster would inflict such harm to a young child?"

A man hollered, "Jeff Davis ought to be whipped himself!"

A woman on the front row rose from her seat and shook a ragged copy of *Uncle Tom's Cabin* at the audience. "Slavery should have been abolished years ago. That poor child! Why, some of his wounds have never healed. He looks as if he were beaten just yesterday!"

He was, I thought. *But not by Jeff Davis.*

We toured for several weeks in this manner until Captain Hudson received correspondence and new orders from Washington. It seemed some prominent abolitionists had taken an interest in Jim Limber and had complained to Washington about the boy's treatment in public. The tour was to end immediately. There were to be no more sideshows. Captain Hudson would place Jim Limber in the care of a local benevolent institution or turn him over to a suitable guardian. Then, the captain was to report for administrative duty in Washington. This news displeased Captain Hudson greatly.

A week later, Captain Hudson hired a hansom. He ordered the driver to take us to the river just outside the city limits.

As we traveled, Jim Limber peered out the carriage window. The moon was full and his eyes latched onto the white orb in childlike awe.

"I bet you my brother Jeff is looking at this same moon tonight," Jim said. "I want to go home. When are you going to let me go back to my family?"

I whispered, "Best be quiet or you'll get another lickin'."

"You can stop here, driver," Captain Hudson said.

The driver remained with the carriage while the three of us walked down to the river. The captain and I returned a half-hour later, our boots sloshing water.

"Where's the darkie?" the driver asked.

"He ran away," the captain said. "Good riddance, too."

That was the last time either of us spoke of Jim Limber.

I awoke from my reverie and looked at the fire. My letter, like all the letters from nights before, was now a thin sheet of gray ashes.

"Leave me be, Jim Limber," I whispered.

But I know he won't.

Manhunter

*There is no hunting like the hunting of man,
and those who have hunted armed men long enough
and liked it, never care for anything else thereafter.*

—Ernest Hemingway

The thunderclap woke Chicolithe. He stretched his legs on the rope bed and listened to a surge of wind as it roared through the pine tops and to the rain as it pounded the wooden shingles and slid from the cabin roof to slap puddles of water on the hard clay ground. It had been raining hard for two days.

He sat up and looked out the cabin's one window by his bed. The thunder echoed through the piney hills like enfilading cannon, and he heard a bolt of lightning crackle high above the earth, and he watched it burn sky and air until it augured its tentacle downward into a pine. A tree split and crashed into the ground. As the storm moved eastward, the thunder eased into rumbles and the lightning into white-charcoal screens. His bluetick hound stirred, and the dog's tail thumped the bedpost. Chicolithe reached down and scratched the animal's head.

"One of them will run tonight, Nimrod, if they ain't gone already. Best get some rest, boy."

The dog blew out a breath, licked Chicolithe's hand, and rested his muzzle on his outstretched paws.

Chicolithe rose an hour later, let the dog outside, and then moved to the stool at the fireplace. He threw pine kindling onto the embers and blew them into flame. The blackened clay of the stick-framed clay chimney was cracked and thick with charred pine resin. The smoke swirled and looped inside its black crypt, then spiraled up the flu into the gray sky. After the logs caught, he let Nimrod back inside and made coffee and a small boiler of cornmeal mush. As he ate, he stared into the flames, his thoughts taking him to earlier pursuits of these erratic and desperate men in blue coats.

He heard the splash of brogans wading through the mud and puddles outside his cabin. A small hand, not a man's fist, pounded on the door. It would be one of the guards from Camp Ford. Slipping his suspenders over his shoulders as he rose, he opened the dilapidated pine-board door. "Come on in, boy. Get dried off. Help yourself to some mush and coffee."

The fifteen-year-old stepped inside, removed his slouch hat, and squeezed the water out of it. "I'd like to eat and visit a while, Mr. Chicolithe, but I got to get back to the fort. Colonel Allen wants you to come right away with your dogs. Some Yankees run away yesterday sometime."

"How many this time?"

"Colonel said a half-a-dozen of 'em."

Chicolithe ciphered the silver dollars he would earn if he could catch them all. "When did they get out?"

"He doesn't know, but it was before evening roll call yesterday. That's when he knew for sure."

Chicolithe poured coffee into a tin cup and handed it to the boy. "Drink yourself a cup of coffee. We got time."

"Thank you, Mister Chicolithe." He blew on the lip of the cup and took a sip. "I'd sure hate to be outside in the woods in this weather." The boy held his hands over the fireplace. "I reckon they thought the rain would cover their trail."

"They thought wrong." Chicolithe studied the boy who had already worked the camp for a year. He was one of about two dozen militiamen on guard duty at Camp Ford—all of them boys, old men, or stove-up soldiers—who guarded the 2,000 Federal troops inside the stockade. If the war lasted another year, this boy would be sure to sign on with regular Texas infantry or cavalry. A couple of the other boys guarding the fort seemed a bit addled and thickheaded to Chicolithe. He doubted they would ever be accepted for regular service, but this boy— he would be absorbed quickly.

A half-dozen. That meant that it wasn't the impulsive blind run of a few soldiers who seized an opportunity, but it indicated a planned escape. Likely, they had weapons and food stored up and a route planned. Maybe they had received help from someone outside the stockade. If the escapees stayed together, they would be easy enough to catch, but if they split up, Chicolithe knew he would have a devil of time catching them all.

"Well, boy, help me load up the dogs, and we'll be on our way. It sounds like the rain is letting up."

While the boy hitched his two mules to the wagon, Chicolithe saddled his horse and tied him to the back. He threw a sack of corn into the wagon bed and checked his guns. When he stepped over to the dog pen, the six hounds inside bayed and pawed the gate. When he swung it open, the bloodhounds swarmed out, noses to the ground, their tails slapping the air in excitement.

"Shut your mouths and get in the wagon," he said.

The dogs sniffed their way to the tailgate and hopped into the wagon bed. "You too, Nimrod," he said. Nimrod, looked at him like an indulgent sergeant major would look at an officer giving orders before a battle, then hopped up with the others, sitting on his haunches in a corner of the wagon bed. Chicolithe released the wagon brake and snapped the reins. "Go on you sorry excuses for mules."

The boy hopped up into the wagon seat with him. "Why do you call that dog Nimrod?"

"Well, when I was a boy, I knew this old Jewish man in Tyler. He used to tell me stories from the book of Genesis. One of them was about Nimrod, whom he called 'a mighty hunter of men before the Lord.' Now this old man says that Nimrod could hunt and track men and animals better than any man on earth. People feared him, and I'd say they had good reason to. I guess Nimrod had to have been a good manhunter if he caught the good Lord's attention. This hound of mine is the best manhunter I got, so I gave him that name, Nimrod.

"He's the smartest and meanest hound I ever had. He'll let a boy in gray pat him on the head, but the sight of a blue uniform seems to make him crazy mad. Must be some kind of natural instinct that some of the human race don't have."

At first light, they happened upon a wagon of refugees—a mother, her young boys, a teenage daughter, and two servants. The wagon was piled high with their belongings. One of the servants wore a Confederate kepi. The servant raised his hand in greeting, and then asked Chicolithe, "How far are we from the town of Tyler?"

"About two miles straight ahead," Chicolithe said. "Where are you folks from?"

"From Louisiana," one of the girls said. "We had a plantation near the Mississippi River. We are the Stone family. My name is Kate."

"Are things as bad in Louisiana as I've heard?" he asked.

"Yes. Yankees, Jayhawkers, and other ruffians have taken over. They're stealing and burning everything. We decided it would be prudent to move to a safer area."

"When you get into town, go to the Methodist church. The minister will help you. He's taken it on himself to help folks like you. He's commander of some sort of refugee relief committee."

"Thank you, sir," she said. "Tyler, Texas." She sighed. "It seems so far from our Brokenburn."

When the pilgrim family moved on, the boy said, "That Kate is a pretty thing. Don't you think so? I just might have to go to town and see her next chance I get. Make sure they get settled and all."

"I wouldn't get your hopes up if you got courtin' on your mind. Ain't no planter's daughter going to be interested in a East Texas ploughboy."

"Well, we'll see about that. Do you have a sweetheart, Mr. Chicolithe?"

Chicolithe spat into the road. "You mind your own business." He popped the reins and the mules plodded forward.

As Chicolithe neared the stockade he reined the mules to a stop. He looked down into the five-acre prisoner of war camp and contemplated the crude makeshift log and earth cabins. Some dwellings were merely lean-tos constructed of scraps of lumber, pine branches, and canvas; some were tarp-covered soddies or shebangs, which were merely holes in the earth covered with tarps. Blue coats, dirty muslin shirts, and a hodgepodge of colors and costumes swarmed like restless ants in the daylight. Red-capped Zouaves with their bulbous britches bobbed about like fishing corks on a pond. His hounds pushed their way to the front of the wagon, peering over his shoulder as if they too wanted to again examine this oddity of architecture and humanity. A bugle sounded for the 7:00 a.m. roll call, and the swarm metamorphosed into lines. One dog growled.

"You settle down, Stuboy. You'll running down some of 'em soon enough." He turned his head and spat a stream of tobacco into the muddy clay road. He popped the reins and said, "Go on, mule."

"Place is swelled up real tight now," the boy said. "All those prisoners they brung back from Mansfield, Louisiana, have durn near filled the place up."

"The possibility that we might take so many prisoners never entered our leaders' minds, best I can tell." Chicolithe said. "You know, boy, I feel sorry for those Yankees in a way. A prisoner of war camp is an awful thing. You take a man out of a soldier's life and stick him in a place like this, you're likely to do something horrible to his insides. I hear it's worse on our boys they took up North. A Southern boy ain't like these Yankees. He don't mind fighting, he can suffer through being hungry and tired and wet and cold, but he just ain't made to be corralled in a situation like this."

Two young guards on picket duty sat along the road. They stood as the wagon approached, and when they recognized Chicolithe, they sat back down. One resumed cleaning his single barrel shotgun, and the other whittled on a cedar branch, the shavings piled up near his feet. Neither boy could have been sixteen.

"You been inside that pen yet, Mr. Chicolithe?" the whittler asked. "It's like a durn circus or insane asylum. The Colonel's expecting you. You can leave the towhead here with us."

The boy stepped off the wagon. "I ain't had breakfast yet."

"You done missed breakfast. Weren't much today noway. Just some fried mush and sorghum."

"It's a long time till supper," the boy said. "Reckon you could get me something to eat, Mr. Chicolithe?"

"If they feed me, I'll ask the Colonel to send some up to you too."

"Much obliged, Mr. Chicolithe."

At the house, two women sat on the porch in rockers. One was an attractive young woman with a book in her hand. The older woman was knitting. When she saw Chicolithe, she set her work in her lap and smiled.

"My husband is expecting you," she said. A Negro was stacking firewood near the house. "Benjamin, would you please step inside and notify Colonel Allen that Mr. Chicolithe has arrived."

"Yes, ma'am," he said.

"This is Mollie Moore, Mr. Chicolithe, a wonderful poet and singer from Houston. She has come to entertain the troops stationed here and the prisoners as well, though the escape last night may have sabotaged their chances for much entertainment. My husband is most irate over their ingratitude."

"I'm pleased to meet you, ma'am," Chicolithe said.

"Mr. Chicolithe is here to recover the escaped prisoners, Molly. He is an expert tracker and marksman. He can follow the faintest of trails, and it is said that he can out-track any Indian in the woods or prairies. His skill is legendary."

"Is that so?" Miss Mollie said. She looked at his dogs. "Your dogs do look like they are vicious creatures."

"I wouldn't call them vicious, but they can put on a ferocious face when they want. Some prisoners say I starve my dogs to make them meaner. That ain't true. They say that I don't allow them to hunt nothin' but a man. That is true. They can follow a scent eight days old, even after a rain. The Yankees call them sleuth-dogs. Like me, my dogs don't care for Yankees none."

"Do you have to use dogs to catch them?"

He reached down and petted Nimrod's head. "No, ma'am, I don't have to use dogs to follow and catch a man, but the dogs do hasten the process. My dogs are hunters like me—they'll follow a man day and night till they get him. You know, when Cortez landed in Mexico, he got the attention and respect of the Aztecs by three things: guns, horses, and his war-dogs. I've got all three, and I've surely got the attention of the Yankees here."

"Ah, a man who knows history. Do you like poetry, Mr. Chicolithe?" Mollie asked. Her eyes were sparkly, playful. He thought her a little arrogant, like she was testing him.

"Lot of folks write poems, ma'am," Chicolithe said. "I like some of what I hear, though most of what people call poetry leans toward the overly sentimental. I do enjoy reading good poetry when I can get it."

"Well, I hope you favor mine. I will look for you at my reading this evening."

Colonel Allen, a captain, two lieutenants, and a civilian came out of the cabin.

"Mr. Chicolithe," the Colonel said, "It seems I am in need of your tracking services once again."

"That's what I hear."

Colonel Allen scratched his neck under his beard and said, "Every batch, there's always a few that starts planning an escape. And I don't know why. I allow them to sell their souvenirs to Tyler folks. I try to feed them decently. They've heard of Camp Groce, they know this is not an Andersonville, and they know that if they go back to fightin' they're likely to get killed or captured again."

"It's hard to explain human nature, Colonel. The ones that try to escape never think it out entirely. I see you've enlarged the stockade."

"I had to. It's a perplexing thing, having all these prisoners. It filled up faster than we had thought, so I had to pull all the logs up, cut them in half and split them and rebuild the fence. And they still keep coming. We've already got prisoners from a hundred Federal regiments and seventeen states, a herd of sailors from the Federal Navy, seven colonels, four majors, forty-eight captains, ninety lieutenants, one doctor and one naval captain. Even got a couple of Texas boys from Jack County who had joined the Federal army."

"I thought you had arranged a prisoner exchange, so you could get them out of here."

"We thought so. We marched them to Shreveport, but the talks broke down, so General Kirby ordered us to march them back. You should have heard them cursing their idiot leaders. One Kansas boy I talked to broke down and cried. He said they couldn't understand why the Grand Army of the Republic cancelled the prisoner exchange. They were most discouraged.

"I must apologize, Mr. Chicolithe. The responsibilities of my position sometimes distract me, and I ramble. Regarding your pay. I'll pay you in Mexican silver coin. One dollar per man that you return."

"The boy said a half-dozen lit out?"

"That is correct. I'm afraid we had a bad storm last night, and they made use of that diversion to slip away. They pried some logs loose on the eastern side of the stockade."

"The stockade looks mighty crowded. My guess is you're about to have a passel of escape attempts. Of course, when I get back with these, maybe the others won't be in such a hurry to get out."

"What do you mean, sir?" a Lieutenant asked.

"I mean that they'll find it's safer there, than when I'm after them. And this camp here…Well, it will seem like a traveler's hotel compared to life on the run.

"They cain't have gone far. If they went due east, like I think they did, they'll slow down when they hit the swamp. Most of them have no sense of direction and will get lost trying to cut through it or circle it. You want them back alive? If I have to shoot one, and if you wanted his body toted back, you'll have to send along some help."

"Live will do fine, but don't put yourself out to make them walk back. I'll send a wagon along the road, and you can have the three guards you met coming in, and a couple of the Twelfth Texas Cavalry that have just been stationed here. These

Federals who escaped were all officers. I can't tell you how important it is that we find them quickly."

"Don't you worry none. I'll fetch them home. As far as men, just give me the towhead. If I need more, I'll send him back to get them. I will need some rope or lariats though."

"As you wish."

Chicolithe walked around the stockade and found where the prisoners had slipped through. Two servants were resetting the logs. His eyes followed the faint trail made by their bare feet and thin brogans. He filled his pipe, popped a Lucifer on a stockade log, and smoked, speculating. He walked around the stockade, looking for other breaches and trails.

At the gate, Chicolithe watched a guard escort a Yankee out of the stockade to the hospital building. A gaunt, walking skeleton, his body wasted away by dysentery, he must have lost his mind somewhere in Camp Ford. He held an ear of corn near his face and talked gibberish to it as if it were a close friend. As far as Chicolithe could tell, the corn's new friend didn't have a grain of sense. He moved on to his wagon. The towhead was already there. Miss Mollie and the Colonel's wife still sat on the porch.

"Well, let's get started, boy," Chicolithe said. He untied his horse from the wagon and mounted. He shouted, "Let loose the dogs of war!"

He glanced up at Miss Mollie and saw her nod approvingly. "I see Mr. Chicolithe knows some Shakespeare. I do so hope that you will be back in time to hear my poetry."

The towhead dropped the wagon's tailgate. Chicolithe's eyes shifted to the visiting poet. "I look forward to hearing your poetry, Miss Mollie."

Chicolithe shouted, "Let's go boys. Sing for them! Sing, Cerberus! Sing, Nimrod! Sing, Stu-boy!" The hounds filed off the wagon and let loose a chorus of barks, bays, and growls and followed him to the escapees' trail. The low murmur of voices and other sounds in the stockade stilled. It became so quiet that Chicolithe heard the shrill cry of a hawk above them. He knew it was good for the prisoners who had lacked the gumption to attempt an escape to see and hear the dogs. There was something about the dogs that frightened them. *And my dogs should frighten them*, he thought.

To the towhead, Chicolithe said, "One of us needs to be on foot to work with the dogs. I reckon that's going to be you. Can you keep up?"

"I reckon so. It beats sitting around this camp all day."

He and the boy followed the dogs, and as he anticipated, the escaped prisoners moved east, right toward the big swamp between Tyler and Shreveport. If they didn't split up, he'd be finished by supper. From his horse he studied the trail. They weren't traveling with great speed. They were either worn out or arrogant.

"Are we close to them, Mr. Chicolithe?" the towhead asked.

"We are. Now, listen to me, towhead. As the sleuth-dogs get closer, those Yanks will stop traveling together and make it ever man for himself, and they'll scatter. Are you listening to me, boy? "They're likely hungry, tired, and eaten up by briars and mosquitoes. The mind of an escaped Federal soldier is a most peculiar thing. Once the dogs start baying, the runners always think the dogs are closer and running faster than they are. Makes them careless. Makes them crazy stupid. They'll get scared and run themselves out. That's just what we want. Keep your eyes open too. When we start catching them, we'll truss them up like a string of haltered horses and you'll lead them along. You follow me slow. Don't untie them, and don't stop; I don't care what they say or how much they whine. They might try some kind of desperate ambush on you. If you think one's going to fight you, or if he threatens you, shoot him with that shotgun of yours."

Chicolithe studied the fringe of the swamp ahead. At the next rise, he saw a blue jacket weaving erratically through the brush, and white arms flailing at the briars and vines. When Chicolithe blew his horn bugle, the dogs raised their voices in a chorus of barks and howls. "Get him, boys!" he said.

A couple of the sight dogs caught a glimpse of their prey and belted out in front of the pack, snarling like berserk Vikings working themselves up into a battle frenzy. A few yards away from its quarry, one sprang into the air, hit the Federal high in the back and knocked him down. The other dogs swarmed onto the fallen Yankee, latching onto arms and legs and pinning him to the ground.

In his peripheral vision, Chicolithe caught a flash of blue moving to his right. Two Federals were attempting to make their way along the cypress brake. "Towhead, you go pull the dogs off this one, and get a gun on the prisoner."

He spurred his horse toward the fleeing prisoners. The men paused at the edge of water then waded out into it.

Chicolithe called out, "Listen to me, boys. That little bit of water ain't goin' to slow the dogs down. In fact they like a swim now and then."

One of the Yankees stopped, faced Chicolithe and hollered, "I'm not going back to that camp!"

"You're wrong about that boy," Chicolithe said. He lifted his rifle and dropped the man.

The surviving Yankee said, "Don't shoot me! And don't sic those dogs on me! Please, don't sic those dogs on me!"

"Alright," Chicolithe said. "You come out here to me, and I'll keep the dogs off you."

The Yankee trudged out of the water and came and stood by Chicolithe's horse.

Chicolithe said, "Put your arms down. You can sit down if you want."

The towhead led his prisoner and the other dogs back to Chicolithe. Chicolithe pitched him a coil of rope. "Hog-tie these two and I'll go get the other three."

From his horse Chicolithe could see other tracks leading into a canebrake. He nudged his horse toward it, figuring that the other three had stayed together. Chicolithe hollered, "You Federal boys in there, you best come out. My name's Chicolithe. I know you heared of me. My dogs done chewed up one of your friends, and the other's lying facedown in the swamp water, trying in vain to recover from getting shot. The other one is waiting up yonder. Y'all are going back—one way or another. Now, I could set the dogs on you, or hell, I could just set fire to the cane and shoot you when you run out. I'll give you a minute or so to decide."

A voice called out, "We're going to come out, Mister Chicolithe. Don't shoot us."

Chicolithe said, "You got any guns?"

"Theodore here has a small pistol, but I think the powder's wet."

Chicolithe heard them arguing among themselves. "What are you doing, holding a durn election? There ain't but one decision to make and that's if you're going to walk out of the cane. I'm in a hurry to get back to camp and have a good supper and hear Miss Molly read her poetry."

Two Federal officers filed out. Chicolithe studied their faces. *A man's face and eyes shows what he is*, he thought. *Try as he might, a man can't hide some things.* As a manhunter, he had seen the whole spectrum of the emotions and mindsets of captives—rage, defiance, fear, confusion, frustration, madness, and despair. Officer or enlisted man, when a man is on the run, his face wears the naked truth of what he is in his essence.

Chicolithe counted the now silent men huddle in front of him. Four, one dead on the water, that made five. One missing. "Where's the other one?" he asked the one who had the most fear on his face.

"I—I—I don't know," he replied. Chicolithe lifted the rifle's muzzle and pressed it against the man's chin. "This is no time to take up the bad habit of lying." Nimrod had frozen like a dog pointing quail, his eyes fixed on the cane. Chicolithe heard his low and steady growl. "Nimrod thinks there's still someone in the cane."

The Lieutenant's eyes widened. "He's still in the cane."

"Get him, Nimrod," Chicolithe said. Nimrod spurted into the cane, the other dogs following his lead. A man's angry voice cursed, and Chicolithe heard him thrashing about in the cane trying to get away from the dogs. The man-voice was swallowed up by the barks and growls of the dogs, and then the curses changed to cries for help.

"It isn't right for you to sic your dogs on him," one of the Federal officers said. "Call them off."

"They do sound like they're getting a mite bit worked up, don't they? You can go get your friend if you want," Chicolithe said. "He should have come out like the rest of you had the sense to do."

Chicolithe waited a minute longer, then whistled sharply. The dogs stopped their attack. He knew they still circled the man, waiting for another chance to attack. Chicolithe heard the man hyperventilating and wheezing. He called out, "You ready to come out of that cane now?"

"Yes."

Chicolithe whistled again and the dogs returned to the man-hunting party. Nimrod rubbed his bloody muzzle on the grass, and then nudged each of the other dogs as if congratulating them for their work.

Chicolithe heard the prisoner trudge cautiously toward them through the cane. He stepped out in the open. His blue jacket was shredded and stained with blood. His eyes were glazed and crossed.

"Lord, have mercy," one of the Union officers said. "He needs medical attention. Can't you put him on a horse?"

"Patch him up best you can. He walked away from Camp Ford. I reckon he can walk back like the rest of you." He lifted his rifle and pointed the barrel west, toward the road. "You boys get to walking that direction. That will put us on the Tyler road and it will be easier walking. We'll follow along right behind you."

"What about that Yank you shot?" the towhead said.

"What about him?"

"Captain won't pay you unless he sees the body, Mister Chicolithe."

"I reckon you're right about that."

Chicolithe backtracked the group to where he had shot the escaping prisoner. The Federals stood at the edge of the swamp in silence, staring at the bobbing blue body, facedown on the water. "Y'all wade out and get your friend," Chicolithe said. "You can bury him back at the camp." He pitched a coil of rope to the ground. I ain't happy about it, but I guess I'll walk back. You can tie his body across my horse."

He allowed the Federals to walk in a clump until they neared Camp Ford, then he tethered them neck-to-neck and ordered them to walk in a single file. Chicolithe called out, "Sing for them, boys!" Nimrod and the dogs began their hunters' chorus—howling, snarling, and barking, as they herded the prisoners forward, nipping at the prisoners' heels like stock dogs.

The Colonel met Chicolithe at the edge of the camp. He angrily eyed the prisoners, and then turned to the manhunter.

"Excellent work, Mr. Chicolithe. Excellent! Come by my cabin and I will pay you for your services. Guards! Open the gate for the prisoners. Make sure you write down their names, for I shall call them later for questioning and punishment."

After the Federal soldiers filed into the stockade, the dogs sat on their haunches outside the heavy pine-log gate.

Chicolithe rode on to the Colonel's cabin, dismounted, and tied his horse to one of the cedar porch posts. There was a pail of water on the porch. He drank two gourds of water, wiped his mouth with his shirtsleeve, and walked back to the stockade. He climbed a ladder and studied the mass of prisoners. A few of the prisoners saw him and pointed his way, whispering to their comrades.

He saw one prisoner, standing as if paralyzed, a pewter spoon in his hand. *That's odd,* he thought. The prisoner's eyes shifted to the man next to him, who held a bulbous rag, cupped in his hand. The one with a spoon vanished into a dugout, and Chicolithe watched the other untie his bundle. A thin stream of dust poured out as he walked along the path the Yankees had named Main Street. The soldier, folded his rag and stuffed it into his pocket, then he too ducked inside the same dugout the man with the spoon had gone into. *They're digging a tunnel,* he thought. *Spoonful by spoonful. Guess it gives them something to do.*

He returned to the cabin where the Colonel, Mrs. Allen, and Miss Molly waited for him. Miss Molly said, "I see Caesar has returned with many captives. I shall later compose a poem as a tribute to your exploits."

"You are too kind, ma'am," he said.

Colonel Allen handed Chicolithe a small sack of coins. "I believe this capture will demonstrate to the prisoners how futile the notion of escape is. Hopefully, we will not need your services in the future. Some of the officers want to hunt for deer or perhaps even a buffalo tomorrow. Would you care to join us?"

"Naw, I reckon I'll stick to hunting Federal prisoners." Chicolithe contemplated informing the Colonel about the tunnel. They had probably been working on their mining for some time. He felt sorry for these Federals in a way—all that work and time expended for nothing. A tunnel meant several soldiers would attempt an escape. He emptied the sack of silver coins in his palm and thumbed them. He wondered how many would make the attempt. At any rate, he knew the Colonel would be calling him again soon.

Scanning the sky, he speculated about future weather. Too much rain would flood or collapse the shallow tunnel. This group wouldn't wait for bad weather. They would escape as soon as they dug past the stockade wall.

Nimrod trotted to Chicolithe and rubbed his muzzle against his leg. Chicolithe scratched Nimrod's ears. "Don't worry, boy. We won't have to wait long. Some of them will be running soon."

Lily

October 1862, Charlestown, West Virginia

I approached General Meagher and saluted. He half-heartedly returned my salute and buttoned the top of his greatcoat. "It's turned damn cold, hasn't it? Well, O'Riley? Did the rebels accept our terms?"

"No, sir. The rebel commander, a Colonel Simpson, asked for time to decide. As directed, I told him he had five minutes. He said, 'Tell your general that if he wants Charlestown, he'll have to come and take it. There will be no unconditional surrender of our forces.' "

"How many soldiers does this Colonel Simpson have?" Meagher asked.

"Our reports indicate about three hundred. I saw flags of Virginia and Maryland units. There was only one artillery unit, the Richmond Howitzers, I believe."

Meagher nodded and rubbed his chin. "The good Colonel and his men should have left with the others. He can't stand against our superior numbers, and he knows that, so I assume he and his men remained only to slow down our advance. The general staff has already determined to shell the town to root them out."

William frowned, rose from his canvas campstool, and closed the writing desk. He handed the letter he had just transcribed to General Meagher. The general reviewed the letter and handed it back to William. "Fine penmanship, William. Make sure the letter is sealed and properly posted. Omit O'Mahoney's name from the address. Have you joined the Fenian Brotherhood, yet, William?"

"No, sir."

"You should think about it. Ireland needs good men like yourself." Meagher folded his hands behind his back and studied the small town of Charlestown in the distance. "It's ironic, isn't it? I formed the Irish Brigade to provide materials and training for our men so that Ireland may one day free itself from the English. In order to accomplish that goal, we have become soldiers of a government determined to crush a movement of independence. Many of the rebels are Irish—many of them members of the Fenian Brotherhood. Someday, we will fight with each other against the British. There's too many Irish in this war, William. And the Irish have a way of attracting suffering like no other people. I want you and O'Riley to deliver another message, this time to Charlestown's mayor. Perhaps the mayor can evacuate his citizens before the artillery opens up on the town."

After William had transcribed the general's new message, we walked into Charlestown. The north wind stung our faces, and the white flag I carried whipped and popped in the strong gusts.

"Tis' a bitter wind today, William."

"Aye. Cuts to the bone."

A rebel lieutenant rode out to the two sentries at the edge of town. The lieutenant reached into his haversack for a plug of tobacco. He extended it to William. "You men are welcome to a chew of tobacco. I'd offer you a cigar, but I have exhausted my supply." He looked at the white flag. "Didn't come to surrender, did you?"

William laughed, took the plug, carefully cut off a sliver and handed it back. The Lieutenant passed the plug on to the two guards with him. William motioned for me to speak.

"No, sir," I said. "We have a message for the town's mayor." William handed him General Meagher's letter.

The rebel lieutenant unfolded and read the letter, then stuffed it into his dispatch case. "I'll take your message to the mayor. I'll return with his reply shortly." He mounted his horse and spurred it into town.

We moved off the cobblestone road and sat on a stump in the yard of a nearby house. It was a grand two-story house, its size and architecture reflecting the wealth and status of its family. I unrolled my poncho and spread it on the ground so William and I could play checkers on the board I had painted on the rubber-coated fabric.

"Michael, do—do you know how Charlestown got its name?" William asked.

"No." I moved the flattened Minié ball across the board. "Crown me."

William laid a flattened bullet on top of my new king. "It was na—named after Charles Washington, the bro—brother of George Washington. His house is here somewhere. He ca—ca—called his home, 'Happy Retreat.' It's hard to believe that our own government's artillery is likely to destroy it."

"You think too much, William. We're soldiers. What happens here is not our worry. The rebels should have left town."

A little girl stepped out of the house. She studied us a moment, then bounded from the porch and hopped into a rope swing suspended from a live oak near us. She looped through the air singing "Listen to the Mockingbird," her long blonde hair flowing in the cold October wind.

"She—she's singing her lit—little heart out," William said. "Hearing her makes me miss my own little ones."

The little girl dragged one foot along the ground to slow the rope's momentum, sprung to the ground, then sprinted toward us.

William greeted her with a smile.

"Are you invading our town?" she asked. "You'll need more soldiers if you are. Where's your rifles?"

"We're he—here to deliver a message, Colleen," William said. "We don't need rifles to do that."

"I'm Irish, but I ain't a Colleen. My name's Lily." Her blue eyes flashed proudly. "What are you doing in Virginia? Shouldn't you be guarding Washington where that mean Mister Lincoln lives?"

"Spunky little gals, these secessionists," I said.

"She—she's Irish. What el—else could she be?" William said.

"You talk funny. I had a cousin that stuttered like you. Is Mister Lincoln really a gorilla?" she asked.

"That rumor is not yet proven true," I said.

She laughed. "I wonder if he's a drunk like our mayor. Well, I don't know that the mayor is a drunk, but Mama says he spends too much time in the saloon, so I suppose that means he is."

One of the Confederate soldiers snickered. "Lily has a gift for gab, don't she?"

"You mind how you talk to me, Mister Pete. Now, all you soldiers wait here. I'll be back in a minute." Lily dashed toward the three-story house, crying, "Josephine, Josephine!"

The Confederates groaned. Pete spat, and then said, "Josephine would be her Nanny. If you think Lily is sassy, just wait. Josephine's got a tongue that can skin a man alive. She ought to be out directly."

"Do you know this girl's family well?" William asked Pete.

"I do. And there ain't a better family in Virginia."

"How long have you been in the rebel army?" I asked.

"Since Manassas. "

"Don't you wish the war was over?" I asked.

"Not near as much as you Yankees do," he replied.

Lily burst from the house and ran back to us. She was panting from her run. "Josephine said she'd be here in a minute."

"Is Josephine your slave?" William asked.

"She's my nanny," Lily said. "We don't call her a slave. She's our servant. I don't like the sound of the word *slave*. Sounds dirty and degrading, like you think we mistreat her."

"If you own her, and tell her what to do, and she can't leave you, doesn't that make her your slave?" I said.

Lily tilted her head, lost in some thought, and then her eyes met mine. "Well, can you Yankee soldiers do whatever you want, or does someone always tell you what to do? Can you quit being a solider any time you get a notion to? If Josephine wants to go somewhere, we let her go if we can. It seems to me like Josephine's got more rights than you do. Your President Lincoln puts people in prison just for disagreeing with him. I know that for a face because he put my uncle in prison just for what he wrote in his newspaper. Josephine disagrees with us all the time, but we don't put her in jail and chains for it."

The Confederates and William laughed.

I felt my face turn red. "That's not the same thing, and you know it."

"Well," Lily said, "I fail to see how giving Josephine to you Northerners would make her more free than she is now."

A young black woman, toting a pail in one hand and a coffeepot in the other, emerged from the house. She shuffled across the yard toward us, her feet plowing furrows through the leaf-covered yard. She set the vessels on the ground, stepped back and wiped her hands on her apron.

"See?" Lily said. "Josephine brought you some coffee and water. It's good water here. My papa dug the well himself. He's a captain, under General Lee. His last letter said he was in Fredericksburg. I hope he doesn't shoot you someday." She handed William the gourd dipper. "But you look like nice men, and I know you must be thirsty, and my mama says that we got to maintain our civility even though we're fightin' against some who don't know the meaning of the word."

William drank from the gourd and passed it to me. "Thank you, Lily." His eyes moved to the servant. "And thank you, Josephine."

The child's use of *civility* rattled me a little. I thought about this parley, about the Lieutenant offering William and myself and the other privates tobacco. I'd seldom seen any Federal officer give enlisted men anything other than curses and disdain.

Lily picked up the coffeepot. "Just because you bloodthirsty Yankees have come to hurt our town don't mean I can't be nice to you. Now, unfasten those tin cups I heard clanging a mile away, and I'll pour you some coffee. Josephine makes the best coffee in the whole world. I put the sugar and cream in it myself."

"What do you want in Charlestown?" Josephine asked.

I blew the edge of the tin mug and took a sip of the coffee. "We've been sent to deliver a message to the mayor."

She eyed us carefully. "Is there going to be trouble here?"

"Yes. We're here to drive the rebels out of town. You best tell your mistress that she should pack what she can and leave."

"Them few secessionist soldiers here may leave, but my mistress won't. We've already talked about it. She says citizens ain't likely to be in danger."

"Leaving's for your own good," I said.

Lily said, "I don't want to go either. My daddy says I'm a princess, and Charlestown's my castle. Our gallant knights will defend me to the last."

"Hmmm!" Josephine said. "You been readin' those fairy tales again, I guess." Josephine took Lily by the hand and looked at us. "Ain't no good going to come of you Federals being here. There's meanness in the air today. I can feel it— Lord, Lord, I can feel it. Lily, you get yourself inside."

Lily mimicked her nanny. "Get yourself inside, Lily. Goodness, everyone is always telling me what to do! Mama tells me what to do, Josephine tells me what to do, and now even the Yankees come around telling me what to do. I'm damn tired of it all."

"Lily!" Josephine snapped. "Your mama would have me wear you out if she heard you talking that way." She glared at the two Confederates. "You been hanging around Mister Pete here too long and done picked up that trash mouth of his." She glared at Pete. "I don't care if you are a cousin of her daddy. You watch how you talk around Miss Lily or I'll take a switch to you, too. Lily, you come inside now and leave these men alone." She turned and shuffled back through the leaf-furrowed yard.

Lily curtsied. "Well, I have to mind Josephine and go inside. But I've enjoyed your company, gentlemen. I'm sure you will have the pleasure of seeing me again." She slapped Confederate Pete's arm.

Pete winced and rubbed his arm. "Ow! Lily, you stop that now. If you ain't yakkin', you're pestering me."

"That's for saying I'm a gabby girl." Then she dashed to the porch. At the door, she turned and called out, "Someday you're likely to miss all my yakkin'."

The mayor rode out with the Lieutenant. He looked down from his horse. "Your general's ultimatum has placed Charlestown in quite a dilemma. I'm not sure if he wants our troops out or the civilians. On one hand, Colonel Simpson says he can't exit with his troops and leave the townsfolk to the mercy of the invaders. On the other hand, he realizes that the presence of the troops will allow your general a just cause to attack the town.

"Tell your commander that I thank him for the warning, but one hour is not enough time to allow a total evacuation of our town. One hour will hardly be enough to notify the people to exit. They need time to gather their possessions.

"Of course," the mayor continued. "I'm sure your generals are aware of this, they may be even counting on it. If they are bent on plunder and occupation, the small number we have here will not repel his forces. However, I would appreciate your asking him to restrain his attack against this civilian population or to at least extend the time allowed us to leave."

"I—I will deliver the request myself, sir," William said. "I don't know about the other generals, but Meagher wishes your city no ha—harm."

"Won't do no good, William," I muttered. "They better get the people out."

"When can I expect a reply from your commander?" the mayor asked.

"The attack will—will begin with artillery," William said. "I guess if you hear that, you'll know he has declined your request."

As we turned to leave, a shell whizzed overhead and exploded near the courthouse.

I looked at the rebel lieutenant. His eyes were fiercely fixed on us.

"One hour, hell," he said. I reckon you boys best return to your lines before your own artillery kills you." He and the mayor wheeled their horses around and spurred them away.

I saw Lily in the third story window of her home, waving a white kerchief. William and I waved to her and then double-timed it down the road toward the Union lines. Before we reached our company, the batteries in the hills began in earnest their bombardment of Charlestown, the cannon spewing and belching fire like brass and iron dragons, the spherical case shot shells hissing over our heads before exploding in the homes and streets of the small mountain hamlet.

* * *

With the explosion of the first artillery shell, the citizens of Charlestown began a frantic exodus. From my position above town, I used binoculars and watched them stream south and to the west. The wagons available filled quickly; horses, mules and oxen were loaded down, and human arms clutched and despondent backs bore bulbous quilt-wrapped bundles as they hurried out of town. All appeared to bear more than they could properly carry. The thin line of rebel soldiers took position on the north side of town. The artillery intensified, dumping exploding shells into the Confederate battle line and hammering the houses and buildings with solid shot until most were pulverized. I saw that some civilians had not left the town, but had closed themselves up in their houses. The Irish Brigade advanced toward the gray line of rebel muskets.

As we advanced, the rebel line faded back slowly. Our company pursued them in a skirmish line that took us past Lily's house. Pete lay facedown on the road where I had last seen him, one hand clutching his rifle's ramrod. Near him, a gray-haired woman was sprawled out on the ground, her clothes singed. Her hands clutched a small wooden waiter filled with broken china and pieces of bread.

A crowd of citizens, and some of our own soldiers, swarmed around Lily's house. William and I dashed over. The oak door had been smashed and pieces of it were strewn to the road. With other men of the Irish Brigade, we entered the room on the first floor and heard the sound of many weeping.

A young woman, dressed in black, paced from one end of the room to another. Refusing the condolences of her neighbors, she sobbed violently, crying, "Lily! Oh, my child, Lily!"

Lily's body had been placed atop the piano. A blood-soaked white quilt covered her. Her still beautiful, innocent, pale face seemed the face of a child lost in the sweet dreams of sleep.

Josephine stood weeping over the child. She lifted a pair of shears and cut a lock of Lily's hair. She wrapped an end with string and then pulled it to her face and soaked the lock of hair with her tears.

William approached Josephine. He swallowed hard, and then asked, "How-how did she die?"

Josephine looked at Lily's body. "I told you, nothin' good would come of you Lincoln men coming here. I said you had nothin' we wanted. Lily was upstairs at the window, watching the soldiers leave town. She was always too curious. " Josephine raised the quilt. "Just look there."

We stared in disbelief at the ghastly sight. A solid shot from our artillery had entered the upstairs window and struck Lily in the left breast, tearing her heart and her arm from her body.

William and I gazed at the terrible wound, at the horror our forces had inflicted upon this little flower, shattered before she could bloom. Josephine's trembling hands covered Lily with the quilt death-shroud, contemplated the lock of hair in her hand, a sad *memento mori*, and then slid it into her apron pocket. We turned and left the room.

Outside, William could restrain his grief no longer and he wept. Wept like only an Irishman can. Wept like the Irish always have when they see the cruel and powerful hand of fate raised against the innocent.

William and I were members of the Irish Brigade. This was our first battle, our first bitter taste of war.

Moses

O liberty, how many crimes are committed in thy name!
— Madam Roland

The six Negroes slipped through the pine forest, their bare and brogan-clad feet as silent as the moonlit shadows that fell upon them. A black woman led them, and as she walked, she grunted and dug her walking staff into the ground with every step. They were in single file except for two, Daniel and Jacob, who walked side by side and lagged behind the others. Every now and again, the woman in front would stop and wait for them to catch up.

Once, she stopped, turned, and pointed her crooked oak rod at Daniel and Jacob. "You two keep up. We got to make it north."

"This don't look like no railroad to me," Daniel said. "I heard we was going out on an underground railroad and that it was faster than even that train that comes by our plantation every mornin'."

"That land ain't your plantation. It's your master's," the woman said.

Daniel shook his head. "Mister Roberts always said it was ours. 'This is your land too,' he'd say. And my daddy said the same thing. 'We got to take care of the land. God loves this land,' my daddy always said. He loved my master too. We worked on a task system. When we finished master's work, everything we earned after that was ours. Some days we had more money in our pockets than the master did."

"Your daddy said so?" the woman said. "Well, after today, it ain't yours no more. I ain't never understood how such nonsense could come out of a man's mouth. My husband was a free man, and he talked the same kind of foolishness. When I decided to run away, I asked him to come with me, and he threatened to tell the master what I wanted to do. So I left him behind, and I'm glad I did."

"My daddy always said—"

"You don't even know for sure who your daddy is. Now, keep up, or I'll throw you myself back into the lion's den of slavery. If it weren't for the fact I got other people with us wanting freedom, I'd leave you to the bounty hunters. They will be on our trail come Monday morning. Their whips and dogs will change that tune you got in your head. Well, we cain't stop. Keep on a going. We got to reach the next station."

"Ain't no one looking for me, Miss Moses. My master's wife said I could go."

She ignored him and pushed on at a furious stride. Daniel whispered to Jacob, "She ain't got no right to talk to me like that. I do for a fact know who my daddy is."

One of the other men whispered, "You best quit talking so much. You'll get Moses riled up."

Daniel studied the black woman leading them. "She ain't a real pleasant woman, sure 'nough. Wonder why they call her Moses?"

"She got a calling to lead us black folk to freedom," the man replied.

They stopped traveling near dawn. It was cold, so Moses ordered Daniel to build a fire so they could boil water for coffee. Daniel used a charred cotton boll to catch the spark from his flint and steel. He wrapped an old bird nest around the char and blew the nest into flame and then set it under a stack of pine kindling. After they had boiled coffee in tin cups, someone threw a dry bush onto the coals. It burst into a great flame, and in that moment of illumination, he studied Moses' face. She had removed her slouch hat, and he saw an indention on one side of her head, like her skull had been mashed in with a brick. Her face was hard with hate, like someone the world has been harsh to. Daniel figured she'd never let the world forget her suffering. He chewed on the hardtack Moses had distributed to the fugitives, and thought about the honey-taste of the manna that the real Moses provided his people.

Moses wrapped herself in a blanket, leaned against a pine, and gazed at the fading stars with the eyes of a mystic. Daniel heard her mumble, "Lord, you been with me through six troubles. Be with me in the seventh." She lowered her gaze and looked at Daniel, the fire planting red beads in her dark eyes. "What did you say your name was?"

"Daniel. My daddy gave me that name after that man in the Bible. The Bible Daniel was a servant too. My daddy said that if I ever got in a lion's den, I should do what Daniel done and just keep praying."

"Your daddy didn't give you that name. Your white master gave it to you."

"My daddy said he give it to me. He's the one who told me that story about Daniel in the lion's den. My daddy would die before he'd lie to me."

"Up north, you can learn to read that story," she said.

"I can read it now. My daddy could read it too."

"Who taught you to read?" she asked.

"Our master hired a schoolteacher and made us go to school. Said he didn't want no ignorant servant who couldn't talk or cipher right. Said we needed to make sure no one ever cheated us. Said every man ought to know how to read the Bible, so when the preacher came through we could read along with him. Told us he wanted to set us free, but the law said we had to learn to read and write and learn a trade before he could do it. My daddy said there was a lot of wisdom to that. A man, black or white, who can't make a living, is nothing but a liability to society."

"If your master was such a good man, why are you here with us?" one of the other men asked.

"My master's dead. He got kilt in Virginia. And my master's wife, Miss Julie, well, she came down with consumption. She told us she didn't see how she could take care of us no more, so she said we ought to look out for ourselves. Then, Jacob here told me about this underground railroad, so I thought I'd go north, get some work and send money and medicine back to my family and Miss Julie. You reckon I can find good payin' work, Miss Moses?"

"Black folk can always find work," she replied. "Finding payin' work ain't always easy to do. "

"Where we headed up north, Miss Moses? Illinois?" Jacob asked. "I'd sure like to meet Abe Lincoln."

"No, black folk ain't especially welcome there yet. Mister Lincoln's too busy to take time with the likes of you anyway."

"What about Iowa?" Daniel said. "Some Yankees came through our plantation last week. They said they's from Iowa."

"No, black folk cain't settle there neither. Iowa's too far west anyway. We're taking you to Washington. I know some people there who will hide you."

"If we're going up north to be free, why do we have to hide in Washington?" Daniel asked.

"They got a fugitive slave law now. We'll hide you in a conductor's house there until I can get you St. Catherine's, Ontario. Then whatever you do or whatever happens to you ain't no concern of mine."

"Where's St. Catherine's?" Daniel asked.

"In Canada. Way up north," one of the other black men said.

Moses slapped the ground with her staff. "Why do you fools have to rattle on and ask so many questions? Just shut up, so I can think."

At dusk, they resumed their journey. They came to Broken Shard Creek. Daniel knelt down, cupped the water with his hand and sipped the cold water. "This here's the best water in the South. We came through these parts once when our master needed to buy some cattle from his cousin. This surely is good water. They got water like this up north, Miss Moses?"

"They do," Moses said. "They got rivers that stream down from heaven. I'm taking you to a land of plenty, flowing with milk and honey."

Jacob knelt by Daniel, cupping the water to his lips with his hands. "That ain't what I heard. I heard it was cold all the time, and that the white people there treat you like you was trash. I know, because my cousin was set free and he went up north. Wasn't long till he came back. He's got himself a blacksmith shop in Savannah now. He's making good money too."

"Well, you heard wrong," Moses said.

Daniel said, "I'm hungry. If I had a shotgun, I'd kill us some rabbits. My master used to send me out all the time with his shotgun so I could kill some. When are we goin' to eat something besides this hardtack?"

"There'll be plenty for you to eat up north," Moses said.

They walked on through the night and into the next morning. Stopping on a hill, they could see a river below them. Moses raised her staff and pounded it against a large rock at her feet, and then she pointed the staff north, across the river. "I've never run my train off the track and I've never lost a passenger. On Jordan's stormy banks we stand! On the other side is freedom. All of you get yourselves across that river and don't look back. Remember Lot's wife!"

They slid down the steep hill to the edge of the creek. One man began singing, "Go down, Moses." It was an old gospel song, one like many of the other songs that Daniel knew by heart, songs that his father and mother had taught him. He thought about his parents, the wooden markers over their graves, and their love of the plantation. Moses and the others waded into the river, but Daniel and Jacob hesitated on the creek's edge. Moses turned and sloshed back out of the water.

Jacob looked at Daniel and said, "Something about this railroad of hers don't seem right."

When Moses reached them, she hissed and said, "You ain't gonna drown. The water's shallow. Git yourself across."

Jacob said, "If you don't mind, Miss Moses, I think me and Daniel are going back home and give the matter of leaving some more thought."

Moses' face twisted into a sneer. "Ain't no goin' back."

"If I'm a free man like you say, I can go back. You ain't my master neither. I ain't about to go from one kind of slavery to another. I'll tell the master I got sick and couldn't get back when I was supposed to, so I spent the night in the woods. I ain't feelin' so good right now, so it's not far from the truth."

Moses reached into her haversack and drew a pistol. "You'll be free or die."

"You're talking like a crazy woman. I ain't goin' on with you."

She pointed the Colt at Jacob's head and pulled the trigger.

"Lord, have mercy, you done killed Jacob! You had no call to do that!" Daniel said.

"Dead Negroes tell no tales." Moses pointed the pistol at Daniel. "Well, you want to stay here with your dead friend, or do you want to go north with us to freedom and prosperity?"

Daniel said, "I reckon I'll go north."

The Hanging of David O. Dodd

Stand fast, good Fate, to his hanging!
Make the rope of his destiny our cable . . .
                              —The Tempest I.1.16

January 8, 1864 Little Rock, Arkansas

The Arkansas River had frozen as hard as a miser's heart. Mary, along with her mother and father, joined the stream of Little Rock citizens crossing the ice-bridge to the grounds of St. John's academy. The snow crunched beneath brogan and boot-clad feet, and the ice-face of the river moaned and creaked beneath the load of melancholy Southerners who trudged toward the Tyburn Tree nightmare.

With children in arms and in tow, the Arkansas pilgrims converged onto the grounds of St. John's College. Outside the stone building, a line of cadets, former classmates of the boy they have come to honor, stand at attention, wordless and weaponless in their white and gray uniforms. The Federal officers had heard rumors of trouble, so, near the gallows, lines of Federal soldiers stood stiffly at shoulder arms, their bayonets fixed. Mary hoped there would be trouble—a riot, an insurrection, something to bring grief to Steele and the 15,000 Federals troops who had invaded Little Rock.

Directly ahead, she saw Minerva, a girlfriend, waving her hand. Mary returned the greeting and walked to her. Minerva wore a heavy woolen black, hooded cape, and with her head bowed and hands stuffed inside a fur muff, Mary thought Minerva looked like a monk.

The two girls, both sixteen, walked to the line of large oaks that bordered the academy. They huddled together like the women who once gathered at the foot of the cross in the

Gospels—another execution carried out by another brutal and powerful government. They spoke of David, of the holiday dances of recent weeks, of secret kisses, and walks under stars and moon. The north wind carried away their whispered words.

A woman's voice called out, "Minerva! You need to join us now."

Minerva coughed and touched her teary eyes with a white handkerchief embroidered along its edges with tiny red roses. "I must return to my mother. She is most upset by David's troubles. She says it's a sign of the end of the world."

"Of our world perhaps."

"How could this happen, Mary? How could they accuse David of being a spy?"

"I don't know, Minerva. I don't know."

"I know you took a fancy to him too, Mary, but it breaks my heart to think of the Yankees hanging David. You don't think he was a spy, do you, Mary?"

"No, of course not."

"Mother says you must go to Vermont."

"Yes. It seems I've been exiled from Little Rock. General Steele practically accused me of being David's accomplice. Father and I will leave the day after tomorrow."

Minerva embraced her and said, "I will miss you, Mary."

When Minerva left, Mary circled the tree until she saw David's initials carved on the tree next to her own. She removed a glove and placed her bare fingers on the letters and she shivered as if she had touched magical runes. "Oh, David," she whispered. "If only you hadn't been such a showoff, writing down everything you saw and thought in that strange Morse code. If only you hadn't copied down what we heard those Yankees saying in my house…" Mary looked again at the gibbet that the Yankees had built that morning. It was constructed of two tall timbers joined at the top by a rough crossbeam. Beneath the crossbeam dangled a thick hangman's noose.

Near the crude gallows, Alderman Henry was engaged in somber conference with a group of Little Rock citizens. With him stood Mr. Walker and Mr. Fishback, the attorneys Henry had hired to represent David.

Mary's father now conversed with two Federal officers who billeted at their house. His eyes met Mary's, and then he turned away. Mary could sense the hurt, disappointment, disgust, and anxiety that he felt. "Daddy," she sobbed, and she leaned against the tree and buried her face in her arm.

A hand touched her shoulder. "Don't you dare cry, Mary," her mother whispered. Her voice was bitter, with an edge sharp enough to cut a Yankee's throat. "David needs you to be strong."

"Daddy betrayed David to the Yankees," Mary said. "And he as much as admitted to General Steele that I was guilty too."

"No, your father's just making sure they don't hang you as a spy's accomplice or send you to Rock Island. The Yankees would just as soon hang a woman as man. You've heard what they've done to women in Alabama and Georgia." Her mother handed her a handkerchief. "Now, wipe your face."

"Will David suffer, Mother?"

"I think not. I bribed one of David's guards to slip him a bottle of laudanum. I pray he took it. Not a word of that to your father."

"Mama, they're sending me to Vermont, like I'm a banished criminal. I don't want to leave Little Rock. I don't want to leave you. Why aren't you going with us? That General Steele is an evil man. The charges against David weren't true, and he knows it."

"Be grateful your father arranged your journey to Vermont. This war has changed *everything*, Mary. It doesn't matter to the

Federal Army what *true* and *right* means. They have their own notions about such things. As far as you being a criminal—it doesn't take much for a Southerner to receive that title. And I have my own reasons for not going to Vermont."

Mary whispered to her mother, "What will they do with David's body?"

"I heard that Barney Nighton and Dick Johnson have been given responsibility for the funeral, and that he will be buried in Mount Holly Cemetery."

Someone shouted, "Here he comes!"

Mary stood on tiptoe and observed a mule-drawn wagon approaching. As it lumbered closer, Mary saw seventeen-year-old David straddling a pine coffin. David's face was placid, serene. He lurched forward each time the wagon rocked out of frozen ruts, clutching the coffin's rough pine boards to steady himself. Two Federal soldiers were also in the wagon, a driver and a guard. The guard's blue-white hands were locked around the barrel of his Springfield and he shook beneath his sky-blue greatcoat like a palsied man.

The wagon crept forward, and Mary listened to the strange rhythm of the breathing of the mules and the crunching sound of the wagon wheels. Mary tried to translate the sounds into Morse and the Morse into words, just like David had taught her, but her heart hurt, and she couldn't concentrate. When the wagon stopped, a phalanx of Federal troops surrounded it on four sides, forming a blue box wall that separated the wagon from the Arkansas residents.

Mary edged closer and called out, "They gave you a cold day to die on, David!"

David searched the crowd for the voice and his eyes found Mary. "Mary, I'm so sorry you have to see this. At least they gave me a coffin. I've heard the Yankees usually just dump an enemy's body into a hole."

The guard in the wagon looked at him.

"Ah, John, you've been a good friend to me. I don't mean to belittle you because you are a Federal soldier."

"I'm not here by choice, you know that. Lincoln drafted me." He spat. "I didn't have no $300 like a bunch of boys did to get out of it. This business today gives me no pleasure, David. I hope you know that."

"I know," David said. "John, you remember Sally I introduced you to last week? Take her out and show her a good time. I know you'll be good to her."

"I will, David."

The other guard, the driver, said, "The captain will put you in stocks if you don't quit talking to a treasonous spy like that."

"You tend to your own business, you ignorant muleskinner," John said. "You ain't got a heavy coat on, David. I don't hardly see how you can stand this cold."

David looked up at the ice-blue sky, then down at the sea of blue coats surrounding the wagon. David's expression reminded Mary of the martyrs in the stained glass windows of the Episcopal Church.

"I'm wearing my burial suit, John," David said. "It's warm enough. First and last time anyone's seen me in it. And after that tonic you gave me, I don't hardly feel the cold. Mostly I feel empty, like I just woke up from a dream I don't understand. Looks like most of Little Rock has come to see me off. I always did like to be the center of attention."

"I can think of less hurtful ways for a man to get attention, David," John said.

David looked down at Mary and smiled. "That girl there is my sweetheart, John."

"The one you told me about? I wish I could get you some time alone with her."

"I wish so too, but I reckon we've already said nearly everything that needs to be said."

David fixed his eyes on the oaks lining the edge of the campus. "I always admired those oak trees yonder, Mary. Remember the one in the middle?"

"Yes," she said. "I remember. I'll always remember."

A soldier tossed down an apple box, and the provost marshal, Reverend Pesk, the executioner, and a military doctor used it to step up into the wagon. "The prisoner will stand on the tailgate," the provost marshal said.

David rose from his coffin-seat and stepped forward.

The provost marshal continued. "We are still willing to commute your sentence to prison if you will name your accomplice."

David looked him in the eye and replied, but a strong gust of north wind drowned out the words.

"What did he say?" Mary asked her mother. "What did David say?"

"I think they asked him to name his accomplice."

"Did he name anyone?"

"No, he did not. Give me your hand, Mary."

Reverend Peck stepped forward raised a Bible and the crowd hushed. He and David bowed their heads. The men in the crowd removed their hats as the minister prayed.

The crowd voiced amen with the minister and the provost marshal barked, "Remove the prisoner's coat and blindfold him!"

Dekay, the executioner, said, "Sir, I didn't think to bring a blindfold."

"We can't hang him without one."

David said, "I got a handkerchief in my coat pocket. You can use that if you're bound and determined to not let me see my last moments on earth."

John removed David's coat, dug into its pocket and pulled out a white handkerchief. He shook it out, rolled it up, and tied it across David's eyes, and then tied his hands and feet with rope.

Dekay lifted the noose to slip it over David's head. A gust of wind, like a telegraphic pulse, pushed David back, as if away from the rope of execution; but like the people surrounding the wagon, even God's wind lacked the power to change the inflexible will of the Federal army who had decreed this day's ceremony. Dekay's cold, blue fingers jerked the boy back to his place, and he fumbled with the rope until it was drawn tightly around the boy's neck.

The provost marshal stepped forward and spoke to David in whispers.

Someone in the crowd shouted, "Better not get too close, Marshal! That little boy might be dangerous! I've never seen such a ruthless killer in all my life!"

Another man shouted, "He's just a boy! Why don't you just spank him and send him home! This ain't right!"

David looked the Provost Marshal in the eye and shook his head. Mary shouted, "If you're asking him again to name his fellow-conspirators, you might as well save your breath!"

"Hush, Mary!" her mother said. "You'll get yourself arrested yet."

Mary closed her eyes as the provost marshal tripped the tailgate latch. *At last, it's over,* she thought. The gasps and shrieks of the crowd jerked her eyes back open. She saw David's body bouncing like a martinet as his toes clawed at the snow-covered ground. She could see the rope burning red streaks on David's neck as he thrashed and flailed about.

Alderman Henry shouted, "The damn fools used a green rope!"

Several others cried out, "Cut him down! Cut him down!"

A captain bellowed, "Sergeant, get a man up that gallows and have him pull on the rope. Have another grab his legs."

Two soldiers knelt and grounded their Springfields. One shinnied up the pole and sat on the crossbeam to pull the rope tighter on David's neck, while the other clamped onto David's legs and pulled downward.

Several women in the crowd screamed when David's neck visibly stretched and his tongue protruded. When David's gargled curses were muted into choking sounds, a Federal soldier fainted, and another vomited. A sergeant kicked the unconscious soldier and cuffed the sick one. "Straighten up, soldier! You babies will see worse before this war's over!"

"This isn't a hanging! It's a strangling!" a man in the crowd shouted. A snowball pelted the sergeant's greatcoat.

For five minutes, the crowd listened to David's death rattle and watched his body jerk and twitch in death throes. After a final convulsion, his body stiffened and stilled.

Mary looked up at the sky, wondering if she would be able to see David's soul ascend to heaven.

The corpulent Federal doctor hooked a finger into David's shirt collar, and pulled David toward him. He checked David's wrist and neck for a pulse, and finding none, said, "You can cut him down. He's dead."

The soldier straddling the crossbeam did so, and David's body thudded to the ground.

"Well, it's done," her father said. "We need to go home now. Come along, Mary." He and Mary's mother turned away to return home.

Mary remained and watched two Federal soldiers lift David's body and pitch it into the wagon bed. John and the driver lifted the corpse and dropped him into the coffin. As if on cue, the bells of Christ Episcopal Church rang—seventeen times.

Mary watched the wagon as it returned to the arsenal where David had been held prisoner. She strode boldly to Mr. Nighton and Mr. Johnson.

"Mr. Johnson, what arrangements have been made for David's funeral?" she asked.

"We'll obtain David's body in about an hour, after the medical officers have examined him. We'll prepare his body and bury him tomorrow. You are welcome to come by my house tonight and view his body to pay your last respects. He'll be buried in Mount Holly Cemetery in the morning. However, only his two aunts and their husbands will be allowed at graveside. And by orders of our illustrious General Steele, no words are to be said at the burial, no songs are to be sung."

"Lincoln's government wants to control us even when we are dead," Mary said. She knew her father wouldn't allow her to visit David's body, and she didn't know that she would want to see his body anyway. The thought of seeing David stretched out on a cooling board or couch depressed her.

"There'll be a reckoning for this someday," Mr. Nighton said. "There will be a reckoning." He offered Mary his arm. "Come, I'll walk you back to your parents."

Mary took his arm and looked back at the Federal troops marching away from St. John's Academy. "I hate the Yankees. I hate every stinking one of them. And I hate my father too for taking me away. Mama hates him too, if she'd tell the truth about it."

"You're an outspoken Southerner, Mary, and I realize that your father is not. But you shouldn't be too hard on him. He only wants to protect you from harm. We could have easily had two hangings today, but even General Steele has qualms about hanging a young girl."

"Why would they do this? David wasn't a spy. He just wrote down what he saw in cipher. Every person in town has the same knowledge. Many people in Little Rock have taken trips for one reason or another. Why aren't we all arrested and tried as spies? What's the difference? Why David? When a boy's father sends him somewhere, he has to obey!"

"David just wrote the wrong things in an odd way."

"He's been writing everything in cipher ever since he worked at the telegraphic office in Monroe. There were many personal notes in his journal that he wrote in code too. Why didn't they read those at his trial?"

"So, you saw his memorandum book? You testified at the trial that you had not."

"There was much I didn't say, Mr. Nighton."

"I see." Nighton patted Mary's hand. "Little Rock is an occupied city. The people over us feel they must use their power occasionally to hurt us, to remind us that we are under their control. If it hadn't been David, it would have been someone else. Sooner or later, one of us would have died to pacify their hunger for violence."

"David's never officially served the Confederate Government. David didn't even want to be a soldier. He just wanted to be a sutler, like his father. He did his best to stay out of the war. He even offered to take the Federal oath of allegiance. They refused his request to die in front of a firing squad. The Yankees gave him nothing. Not even a dignified death."

"Fate wouldn't allow David to be uninvolved. Fate decreed that the cable of his life and his death would be forever linked with the Confederacy. Mary, his death may be more significant to our cause than any of us realize."

* * *

Knowing that David's laughter would never be heard there again, Mary felt a sad emptiness when she returned home. That evening, the Federal officers billeted in Mary's home were jocular as they sipped sherry and smoked cigars with her father before supper. A new officer had been assigned to Mary's house. He said he was an aide to General Steele, and Mary noticed that he had hung his document pouch carelessly on a wall peg. He rattled on about Vermont, about its beauty, and about how certain he was that Mary and her father would enjoy their time there.

Mary remained aloof during supper. The new soldier did not yet know of Mary's alleged involvement and chattered on about the hanging. He had been with General Steele when the physician's official report had arrived. The report said that David had died of a "ruptured spine." He stood and raised his glass of sherry. "To General Steele, and the poor lad's ruptured spine."

"Here, here!" the others said and raised their glasses. Mary did not raise hers.

"David had more of a spine than any of you Yankees do, that's for sure," Mary said quietly. "So, I drink to David Owen Dodd, but not to General Steele." She drained her sherry and resumed eating.

Her father slammed down his fist, so hard that it rattled the silver and dishes on the table. "You will be silent about that boy! And I'll not tolerate your rudeness toward our guests. Perhaps you should leave our company until you can behave in a more civil manner."

Mary stood and pushed in her chair. "Gentlemen, I bid you goodnight."

The soldiers stood politely until she had ascended the stairs. Once safely in her room, she sat at her writing desk, lit a candle lantern, and again read David's letters that she had concealed in a drawer of the secretary. She lovingly lifted the one photograph she had of David, one taken at the last Christmas dance, and she whispered, "I'll always remember you, David Owen Dodd. I'll always love you."

She opened her journal, one exactly like the one she had given David, and read. She found the damning entry in her diary:

The 3rd Ohio Battery has four guns. Brass. 11th Ohio Battery has six guns...

Yes, that is correct, she thought. *Oh, David. I wish I had not teased you into copying this into your own journal in code.* Mary dipped her quill into an inkbottle, turned to the next blank page and wrote furiously. She wrote an elegy for David. She called it, *Boy Martyr of the Confederacy.* Then, on another page she vented the anger she felt for her father. After that, she wrote a sarcastic letter to General Steele, followed by insulting letters to each of the family's Federal boarders. *If I knew I could get away with it, I'd slash their throats tonight while they sleep,* she thought. She also wrote a letter to General Fagan, C.S.A, in Camden, telling him about David's death, about her exile to Vermont, and apologizing for her tardiness in getting him the information he had requested. She felt certain that the general would grieve—both for David and for her. She looked again at David's photograph. She thought, *I'll commune with David's ghost, and as long as I live, I'll remember what the Yankees did to him. They are truly weak when they fear a boy just because he knows telegraphic characters.*

She determined to examine the new boarder's document pouch later that night, when the household had fallen asleep. Surely there would be some valuable information inside. Information General Fagan would value and use, more information that would make David's death meaningful. Tomorrow she would send General Fagan the letter through another trusted friend—just like she had tried to do with David. This time, maybe General Fagan would receive it.

The Yankee in the Orchard

My name is Lucinda Johnson. We live along Bayou Rapides on the same land that my Confederate ancestors farmed. I was named after my great-grandmother

I remember Robert E. Lee toasting the women of the Confederacy in *Gods and Generals*, about how important they were to the cause, to the soldiers fighting. And it's true. It was true then, and it's still true today. Men need the support of their sweethearts and wives and mothers. Most think that the War Between the States was only a man's war, but it wasn't. It was also a war against the women of the South.

There's a bit of ground in our pecan orchard near one of the oldest trees. One day, our dog, a Catahoula cur, did his business there and my mother started laughing. "He knows," she said. "My God, that Yankee hating dog knows."

"Knows what?"

"He knows what's buried there."

"Buried? There? What on earth are you talking about?"

"That's the spot where your grandmother and great-grandmother Lucinda buried a Yankee soldier."

"Did he die on our land or something?" I ask.

"Oh, yes. Your great-grandmother Lucinda shot him."

"Why?"

She just looked at me with those sad eyes that mothers can have sometimes, eyes that probe and teach at the same time. I wondered what this tale would tell me about my namesake.

"He did things to women in these parts that a man ought not to do."

"Oh," I said. I had heard the stories of the rape of Southern women by Federal troops, but these stories were difficult to absorb and process mentally and emotionally. And the more sensitive and Christian one is, the more difficult the acceptance that such things could have happened and the greater the discomfort. I knew Lincoln had waged war on the civilians of the South, but the ramifications of such atrocities coming so close to my own family shocked me.

"Was she or grandmother raped?" I asked.

"No, but several other women in the area were. He came here for that purpose, but it didn't work out exactly like he had expected. Do you want to hear the story?"

I nodded my head.

"It was early 1865, I think she said it was February. Likely, it was, because she said there wasn't much to eat. The Federal troops had occupied Alexandria, thousands of them. There were some units that called themselves *foragers*. Some folks called them *bummers*. Basically, they were rogue thieves who took anything they wanted. They took our food, our money and other valuables, our livestock, and what they couldn't take, they often destroyed or burned, especially if they had been drinkin', which they did every chance they got.

"One officer took a liking to Southern women, and he started taking every one he wanted—black or white. One of the neighbors he ravished was never the same afterwards. Lost her mind, she did. He was the sort of man who is filled with meanness. He reminded your grandmother of a feral dog. There weren't any men to protect them, and if a servant tried to stop him, well, he would just shoot him, too.

"This officer showed up here with his men, threatening and accusing your grandmother of aiding the Rebel forces. Your grandmother was a comely young woman, and he caught a sight of her looking out the window.

'That your daughter?' he said.

'Yes. Why do you ask?'

'I think I'd like to talk to her privately,' he replied. 'In the house.' He looked your great-grandmother up and down. 'Maybe you too.'

"Your great-grandmother glanced at the other soldiers. 'And them? Reckon you can send them on their way? I'll pour you a good glass of whisky."

'That is mighty polite of you. I'm surprised my men didn't find it.'

'I am too, since they seem to have taken everything else,' she replied. 'But I do have some whisky hidden away your men didn't find.'

"Well, he sent his troops back to Alexandria, tied his horse to the porch post and stepped inside.

'Where's your daughter?' he asked.

'You just be patient. Seat yourself. Let me get you something to eat. Maybe if I'm nice enough to you, you won't do what you got on your mind.'

"He laughed and sat down in that same rocker you're in. Well, Grandmother Lucinda went into the kitchen and returned with a double barrel shotgun. 'Get outside,' she said.

"He stood up and said, 'You will regret this.'

'The only regrettin' will be on your part. Now, get outside.'

"She marched him out into the yard, and then she shot him dead. She called your grandmother and they dragged him out into the orchard and buried him. She took the horse and set him loose around Henderson's Hill." She looked over into the orchard. "He's still there, that Yankee officer, buried with all his equipment in a shallow grave."

I thought about that story all night. The next day in my college speech class, I made a presentation about the strength and independence of Southern women. After class, a boy who had pestered me the whole semester came on to me again. He called himself Billy. As we filed out of the classroom, he slipped his arm around my waist and pulled me against him.

"Girl, I just might have to get me some of that," he said.

His breath was sour, and he reeked of stale cigarettes. His leering, arrogant face sickened me. Katy, one of my girlfriends, had gone out with him. He had stalked and harassed her until she agreed to a date. The experience had traumatized her so badly that she quit school and still couldn't talk to me about it without weeping.

"Where are you from?" I asked. I peeled the cretin's arm from my waist like it was a dirty napkin.

"New York City," he said.

"Well, you're just flat out of luck. We Southern girls like men who practice chivalry. Do you know what chivalry is? I'd be surprised if you could even spell it."

I quickened my pace so I could distance myself from him, but he grabbed my arm.

"I followed you last Friday. I know where you live," he said. "In a farmhouse along the Bayou Rapides Road. It seemed to be a really isolated place. I might just have to pay you a visit. You'll change your tune about me. I don't take no for an answer. Ask your friend Katy."

I know my face turned red at his implications. I felt a mixture of anger and defiance—and yes, a little fear. An image seated itself in my mind—me sitting in the old rocker with my dad's shotgun in my hand, the Catahoula Cur doing his business on a strip of freshly dug earth next to the other Yankee in the orchard.

"I'd really think about that if I were you," I said. "Are all guys in New York City as obnoxious and stupid as you? Get lost."

That evening, as I did my chores, I contemplated this house I loved so much. As I swept its cypress-board floor, I thought about how it had once been muddied by the boots of Yankee intruders. I walked through the pecan orchard, thinking of these beautiful trees that somehow, like my ancestors, had escaped ruin during the War. The trees, silent witnesses to the execution of a rogue Yankee, were what Southern women were and are— strong enough to weather the worst of storms, fruitful, and resilient.

"Lucinda! You've got a phone call."

"Who is it?"

"Someone named Billy. He said to tell you that he's on his way over. He sounds thick-tongued, like he's drunk. What do you want me to tell him?"

"Tell him he's not welcome."

My mother came out of the house, the wooden screen door slamming shut behind her. She wiped her hands on her apron, and joined me under the trees. "I told that boy that he shouldn't come out. He said he's coming anyway. Said that you wanted him to come out. I don't like him."

"I don't either," I replied.

"Your face gives you away. Something's heavy on your mind. What are you thinking?"

"I'm thinking about my friend, Katy."

I studied the patch of ground covering the Yankee's bones, and then I went to the shed and found the shovel and leaned it against the wall. I went inside the house, lifted my father's double-barrel shotgun from the gun rack, loaded it with buckshot, and put it in my bedroom. When I saw Billy's car approaching, I said, "When he gets here, try to send him on his way. If he won't leave, you can send him inside."

I went into my room, turned on some music, set the shotgun in my lap, and waited.

Freedom: An Allegory

I wish that the bald eagle had not been chosen as the representative of our country, he is a bird of bad moral character, he does not get his living honestly, you may have seen him perched on some dead tree, where, too lazy to fish for himself, he watches the labor of the fishing-hawk, and when that diligent bird has at length taken a fish, and is bearing it to its nest for the support of his mate and young ones, the bald eagle pursues him and takes it from him...Besides he is a rank coward...He is therefore by no means a proper emblem for the brave and honest....

—Benjamin Franklin

James and his family were servants on a small plantation along Bayou Rapides, not far from Alexandria, Louisiana. He was seven years of age when his mother died of fever in 1861. His father died a year later, shot by a Federal cavalryman when he wouldn't relinquish his master's one remaining horse to rogue foragers. The master's wife called on a freeman, a black minister with a small congregation in Alexandria, to oversee his father's burial. James listened to the man of God read a few scriptures and lead the other servants in "Poor Wayfarin' Stranger," a favorite song of his father. Ruth, the black nanny for the Messer children, took James' hand and squeezed it.

"You listen to this man, child," she said. "Your mama and daddy have gone to a better place now. This war ain't going to hurt them no more. You be strong. Show yourself a man, and make your daddy proud. He's looking down from heaven, and he'll still watch over you."

When the minister finished the eulogy, the other servants lowered the rough, pine-board coffin with ropes into the hole, and then picked up shovels. At first, the coffin resonated like a drum when the gravel and earth struck it, but soon there was only the sound of shovel blades slicing into earth and the dull thud of dirt upon dirt. The servants packed down the mound of dirt with their feet and shovels, and the servant's friends and masters each laid a flower by the carved wooden grave marker.

James saw a button on the ground near his father's grave. He picked it up and studied the tarnished brass. One of the Federal foragers must have lost it. Most of the shine was gone, but he could still make out the form of an eagle, its regal head turned to the side, a shield on its chest, the bird's talons clutching arrows and an olive branch. James had seen this same emblem many times recently—on coins, on the flags and breastplates of marching Federal soldiers.

William Messer was the same age as James. They often played together and sometimes worked together in the fields. After the funeral, William found James. He held a carrier he had made of small stalks of cane. Inside the small cage was a rabbit.

"Mama gave me a little money, so I brought you a gift, James—a rabbit."

James studied the rabbit. "You want me to wring his neck and clean him out now?"

"No! He's a pet. I thought that when we've finished our work for the day, he'd keep you company and comfort you."

James smiled. "Thank you, Mister William, thank you. He sure is a pretty thing."

"Now, you'll have to take care of him—feed him, give him water. He's real gentle and seems used to people, so I think you can take him out of the cage now and then and play with him."

"So, I don't have to keep him in his cage? Can I just set him loose?"

"No, you don't have to keep him in his cage, but you got to keep your eye on him. He might try to run off, and he don't know how to take care of himself like a wild rabbit does."

James didn't like the cage, but he didn't say so.

"Well," William said, "I have to go back to the house and help mama make some more of those tallow candles. She wanted you to walk down to the Smith place and see if they had any wicks or string they could spare."

"Can I take my rabbit?"

"Sure. I can't think why not."

James strolled toward the Smith farm. He stopped at the edge of a small stream, about a mile from his destination. "I'm going to name you, Freedom. Yessir, you's going to be Freedom the rest of your life."

He set the cage down, set himself down, and leaned against the tree. Freedom looked up at him, wrinkled his nose, and hopped back and forth in the cage. James looked up at the blue sky and saw an eagle soaring high above him, flying with power and purpose. In loops and slowly descending spirals, he navigated himself toward the earth. As the bird drew closer, James could see the tail feathers moving back and forth, up and down as he maneuvered himself through the air. It was a large, powerful bird, with a wingspan of nearly three feet. His neck was extended, and he glided downward to the next thermal, and then allowed that draft to push him up again.

Then, the eagle perched himself at the top of a pine tree, spread his wings, and preened itself with its yellow beak. His white head and tail feathers glowed in the Southern sun. James thought its wingspan to be as long as a man's grave, six or more feet.

I didn't know an eagle could get that big, he thought. *Why, I'd guess that he could tote me off if'n he wanted to bad enough.*

James stuck his fingers in the cage and rubbed the rabbit's ears. "They say the eagle is the bird of freedom. That's a good sign, for us, Freedom. He's come to watch over us."

A cottontail hopped through the briars along the creek. The sight of the rabbit gave James an idea. Why not give his rabbit freedom? Freedom belonged to him, and he could keep him or set him free as he pleased. "You want out of your cage, Freedom?" He unhooked the wire catch, opened the lid, and slid his hand under the rabbit's belly. He lifted Freedom and set him in his lap, stroking his soft, thick fur.

He set Freedom down, and the rabbit hopped cautiously about. James picked up the wicker cage, ripped it apart, and threw it to the ground. "I likes you, Freedom. Likes you a lot. But now you's free! There's lots of other rabbits here, and there must be all kinds of food for you to eat." He pushed him toward the wild cottontail. "You go on now."

Freedom sniffed the air, nibbled at a blade of grass, and then hopped toward the other rabbit. A moment later he hopped back to James, and set himself on one of the sides of the broken pet carrier. James wondered why the rabbit didn't want to leave him. If his master set him free, he'd be gone in a minute.

James heard the shrill cry of the eagle before it descended from the sky with blinding speed. As it flew by him, he heard the swoosh of its wings. The murderous eyes of *Haliaeetus leucocephalus alascanus* turned as if to contemplate James, but there was no shield of liberty on its chest, and its yellow talons, already extended in anticipation, held no olive branch. The eagle snatched Freedom from the ground, its talons piercing the rabbit's soft fur, and blood streamed from Freedom's wounds.

"No!" James shouted. James wept as he saw Freedom carried to the North.

A Prayer from Little Round Top

J im leaned his back against an oak to catch his breath, and used its broad trunk as a shield while he reloaded. Bullets bored into the tree, chewing off chunks of bark and notching its edge until the side of the tree resembled a saw blade. The torrent of lead dug into the ground about him, and the Minnie balls slashed branches and saplings and brush, and ricocheted or flattened against rocks. *At least there's a breeze,* he thought, and he sucked a deep breath into his lungs. *It's Southern air,* he thought. *Blowin' my way.*

He watched his friend, Sean, scramble to the left of him in bare feet across the slick, moss-covered rocks, his Enfield slung across his back. The hillside was steep, so Sean's hands clutched branches and bushes to steady his ascent until he too found a shield-tree. Even over the rifle shots and the distant cannon, Jim heard Sean wretch.

He and Sean had woven their way to this point through the boulders and trees, past the dead, past their own wounded friends, relatives, and comrades who would be abandoned to the Federals' mercy if the battle were lost. Behind them, black-powder smoke crept along the ground like a malignant fogbank, veiling the blood staining the moss and leaf-covered ground and congealing in puddles on rocks. Giant boulders rose above the clumps of slain men like tombstones.

Like the other soldiers of the Fifteenth Alabama on this Pennsylvania hilltop, Jim coughed and gagged and choked on his swollen tongue. He licked his parched and split lips, wishing he had a canteen. Hours before, the captain had gathered all their empty canteens and sent a squad of men to fill them. The squad had not returned, meaning that they had been caught in a firefight or had been captured. He and the other men of the Fifteenth had now gone six hours without water, and the heat had steadily increased. Many men had fallen out due to heat exhaustion. Having already taken heavy losses, Colonel Oates was now left with only 400 men and officers to make this crucial assault on the Federal flank.

Jim tore open a cartridge with his teeth, and the acrid taste of the powder only made his dry mouth pucker even more. He emptied the powder into the barrel, squeezed in the cartridge, and rammed it home. Jim rolled down the hill to get closer to Sean, then called out, "Who are we facing, Sean?"

"The green uniforms are Vermonters. I think the blue are Maine men."

"Those Vermonters are crack shots. They've got the eyes and patience of hunters."

"Aye, that they do."

"Where's Sergeant O'Connor?" Jim asked.

"Ahead of us."

"He's a fierce man."

"Aye, there's no fiercer Irishman for sure."

Jim studied the side of the mountain, littered with the scattered forms of his comrades in their Tuscaloosa gray uniforms. *We've got the Yankees on the run, but many of us are going to die here*, he thought.

"Well, you rested up enough to move closer?" Sean said.

"Aye, Sean." Jim picked out a tree, about fifteen yards ahead. He blew out his breath, doubled over and ran to it. A green uniform rose on the summit, and some lines from Sir Gawain floated through his consciousness. He raised his Enfield, steadied its barrel against the tree, and fired. The green uniform tumbled backwards. He fumbled inside his cartridge pouch for another bullet.

The rifle fire from both sides intensified—Spencers, Sharps, Enfields, Springfields—and he heard bullets pass overhead in waves of muffled sound. A rebel yell echoed as the rapidly thinning ranks of the 15th rallied and neared the summit. He marked and started for another boulder a few yards in front of him. A lead fist burned its way into his chest and knocked him on his back. *Damn good shots, those Vermont boys,* he thought.

He closed his eyes. Ellen's face materialized, and he wondered how she would take the news of his death, wondered if she would know, wondered who would win this battle. *Ellen, I love you so much. God Almighty, I do.* And, as he always did in moments of stress, he thought of his sister. He reached into his canvass haversack and his shaking fingers found Sarah's small daguerreotype. He looked at the image of his twin, and he saw her as he liked to remember her, before the famine and the sickness, before they had locked her from his sight in the coffin.

Through his blurred eyes he could make out the blue-tinted outline of Big Round Top about 1,000 yards away. The mountain's base was shrouded in smoke. A Federal in the signal corps stood on its bald, weathered cap and flagged some distant artillery, and heat waves refracted the man's form and the blue haze of the sky. He remembered contemplating the two Round Tops as they marched on the double for this attack. The two rounded mountains seemed like stiff sentinels in the gently rolling hills of Pennsylvania, stone children spawned by ancient volcanoes in a forgotten turbulent age.

"Jim!" Sean called out. "You going to make it?"

"Leave me be, Sean," he said. His throat was so raw, and his voice gargled from the blood in his lungs, so he didn't know if Sean understood or even heard him. He willed himself to shout, "You best watch yourself, Sean! Don't let them get you in their sights."

Some gray forms scurried past him like ghosts. The specters made their way up the mountain, pushing the green-coated Vermonters farther back.

"Gray ghosts. Ghosts, we all are," he said. "We fought our way up here as men, but we'll all leave as ghosts."

"What did you say, Jim?"

Sean had found him.

"Here, take a drink. I took this canteen off a dead Yank." He propped Jim's back against a boulder and held the tin canteen to his lips. Jim felt the hot water in his mouth, but his tongue was too swollen for him to swallow and the water and a trickle of blood ran down his chin.

"Ah, hell, Jim," Sean said. Sean ripped open his sack coat. Jim heard the brass buttons pop loose and roll into the leaves. "You're hurt bad, Jim." Sean yanked a piece of cheesecloth from his own haversack and pressed it against the wound.

Jim pushed Sean's hand away. "Go on and get some Yanks, Sean," Jim said. "Ain't nothin' you can do for me. There's a letter in my haversack. Take it to Ellen, would you?"

"You can give me the letter now, but you'll give it to her yourself. She's a fine woman you intend to marry, Jim."

"Aye, she is." Jim willed his arm to dig in his haversack and his blackened fingers found the letter and its brown wrapping-paper envelope. "I think I saw Sarah last night, Sean. She come to me in a dream again."

"Your sister? Quit talking nonsense. Don't you go and die on me, Jim. We're pushing the Yanks off this mountain. I'll come back and get you. You sit here and rest. You ain't done in yet."

Jim watched Sean move with the other gray men up the mountain to battle with the swarm of Federal sharpshooters, heard the blistering fire descend upon them, knew from the roar of rifles that the Federals had been reinforced, knew now that the battle for this mountain would end in the retreat of the 15th Alabama.

"Jim," a girl's voice said.

He knew the voice. "Sarah?" he said.

The ground moved beneath him, the universe tilted wildly and a swirling collage of images and sounds floated through his head. The images and thoughts took him to his childhood. He imagined himself on their Ireland farm as a young boy, the mountains of Connemarra in the distance. He saw their stone and earth house and the stone fences in the fields about them. Inside the house, Sarah sat in his father's lap, and he heard his father singing, "The Rose of Tralee," heard the weeping at his sister's grave, heard his own last sobbing goodbye to her there. He remembered the hole in his heart when she died, the hollow void he had carried since her death.

For a moment he was again a seasick, heartbroken boy in the hold of the coffin ship, then a young man working at his uncle's farm in Alabama in fields of cotton and corn. He saw himself in the queue to enlist on the day the bells ran. The images and memories called him home to Ireland again, and he wanted to go there forever. He closed his eyes and he heard ocean waves in the bay breaking against the shore. *At last,* he thought. *I'm going home.*

"I'm here, Jimmy," the girl's voice said again. He opened his eyes. Sarah held out her hand.

He raised his hand, and his fingers found hers. "I've thought about you every day, Sarah. I've carried your face in my heart."

"I know, Jimmy." She pulled his arm. "Let's run, Jimmy! Like we used to. Run free with me now."

A gentle breeze nudged him. He took a breath and said, "Let's be on our way, Sarah."

She laughed, as she used to before the sickness came, and he rose and they ran together to the edge of the bay. And the sounds of battle faded in his brain, and as he breathed his last, all he could hear was the waves breaking in the bay and the sound of Sarah's laughter.

Acknowledgements

I would like to extend my appreciation to Booklocker, and especially to Richard and Angela Hoy, for their hard work and help in the publication of this book.

I am very grateful to Jed Marum, (http://jedmarum.com/) an extraordinary Irish musician, for his friendship, research, and the inspiration I gained from his ballads to write "Lily" and "A Prayer from Little Round Top."

I want to thank Ted Brode and the many other fine members in the Sons of Confederate Veterans and the Daughters of the Confederacy for their ideas, encouragement, photos, and the research materials they supplied and helped me obtain. The members of these organizations are true foot soldiers and guardians of history, and their diligence will insure that the stories and facts of the past will not be lost to political agendas and historical revisionism.

And I especially want to remember the many nameless Southern soldiers and civilians who suffered so much during and after the War Between the States. Most of all, it is your story I wanted to tell.